Elfriede Jelinek was born in the Austrian alpine resort of
Mürzzuschlag and grew up in Vienna, where she attended
the famous Music Conservatory. The leading Austrian
writer of her generation, her other works include
Wonderful, Wonderful Times, *Lust*, and *The Piano Teacher*,
now a prize winning film (all published by Serpent's Tail),
as well as plays and essays. In 1986 she was awarded the
Heinrich Böll prize for her contribution to German
language literature, and in 1998 she received the
prestigious Georg Büchner Prize for the entirety of her
work. In 2004, she was awarded the Nobel Prize for
Literature.

women as lovers

women as lovers

elfriede jelinek

translated by martin chalmers

Library of Congress Catalog Card Number: 94-67713

A complete catalogue record for this book can be obtained from the British Library on request

The right of Elfriede Jelinek to be identified as the author of this work has been asserted by her in accordance with the Copyright, Designs and Patents Act 1988

Originally published in German in 1975 as *Die Liebhaberinnen* by Rowohlt Verlag GmbH

First published in English by Serpent's Tail
an imprint of Profile Books Ltd, 3A Exmouth House
Pine Street, London EC1R 0JH
Website: www.serpentstail.com

Phototypeset by Intype, London
Printed by CPI Antony Rowe, Chippenham, Wilts

This translation received financial support from the Commission of the European Community, Brussels

10 9 8 7 6 5 4 3

foreword:

do you know this BEAUTIFUL land with its valleys
and hills?
in the distance it is bounded by beautiful mountains.
it has a horizon, which is something many lands do
not have.
do you know the meadows and fields of this land? do
you know its peaceful houses and their peaceful
inhabitants?
right in the middle of this beautiful land good people
have built a factory. its low corrugated aluminium
roof makes a beautiful contrast to the deciduous and
coniferous forests all around. the factory is tucked
into the landscape.
although there is no reason for it to be tucked away.
it could display itself.
how fortunate that it stands here, in beautiful surroundings and not somewhere else, where the
surroundings are not beautiful.
the factory looks as if it were part of this beautiful landscape.
it looks as if it had grown here, but no! if one looks
at it more closely, one sees: good people built it.
nothing comes of nothing after all.
and good people go in and out of it. afterwards they
pour into the landscape, as if it belonged to them.
the factory and the plot of land beneath it belong
to the owner, that is, a company.
the factory is nevertheless happy, when happy people
pour into it, because they do more work than
unhappy ones.
the women, who work here, do not belong to the
factory owner.

the women, who work here, belong entirely to their families.

only the buildings belong to the company. so everyone is satisfied.

the many windows sparkle and flash like the many bicycles and small cars outside. the windows have been cleaned by women, the cars usually by men.

all the people, who have come to this place, are women.

they sew. they sew foundations, brassières, sometimes corsets and panties too.

often these women marry or they are ruined some other way.

but as long as they sew, they sew. often their gaze wanders outside to a bird, a bee or a blade of grass.

they can sometimes enjoy and understand the nature outside better than a man.

a machine always makes a seam. it doesn't get bored. it performs its duty, wherever it is put.

each machine is operated by a semi-skilled seamstress. the seamstress does not get bored. she too performs a duty.

she is allowed to sit. she has a lot of responsibility, but no overview and no long view. but usually a household.

sometimes in the evening the cycles cycle their owners home.

home. the homes stand in the same beautiful landscape.

contentment flourishes here, one can see that.

whoever is not made content by the landscape, is made completely content by children and husband.

whoever is not made content by landscape, children and husband, is made completely content by work.

but our story begins somewhere else entirely: in the city.

a branch of the factory stands there, or rather, the headquarters of the factory stands there and the place in the foothills of the alps is the branch factory.

here too women sew, which they like.

they don't sew what they like, but sewing in itself is already in the women's blood.

they only need to let this blood out.

this is peaceful women's work.

many women sew half-heartedly. the other half of their heart is occupied by their family. some women sew with all their heart, it is not the very best who do that.

our story, which will soon be over, begins in the urban island of peace.

if someone experiences fate, then not here.

if someone has a fate, then it's a man, if someone gets a fate, then it's a woman.

sadly life passes one by here, only work remains. sometimes one of the women tries to join the life that's passing by and to chat a little.

sadly life then often drives off by car, too fast for the bicycle. goodbye!

beginning:

one day brigitte decided, that she wanted to be only woman, all woman for a guy, who was called heinz.

she believes, that from now on her weaknesses would be strengths and her strengths very much hidden.

heinz, however, does not see anything endearing in brigitte, and he finds her weaknesses only repellent.

now brigitte also takes care of her appearance for heinz, because if one is a woman, one can no longer turn back from this path, and one must take care of one's appearance. brigitte hopes that the future will thank her one day by letting her look younger. but perhaps brigitte doesn't have any future at all. the future depends entirely on heinz.

when one is young, one always looks young, when one is older, then it's too late anyway. then if one does not look younger, the judgement of the world is merciless: did not make cosmetic provision when young!

so brigitte has done something, which will be important in future.

if one has no present, then one must make provision for the future.

brigitte sews brassières. if one makes a short seam, one must make a lot of them, forty at any rate is the absolute minimum piece rate target. if one makes a longer, more complicated seam, one has to make correspondingly fewer. that is very humane and just.

brigitte could get many workers, but she wants to get the one and only heinz, who is going to be a businessman.

the material is nylon lace lined with a thin amount

of foam rubber. her factory has many market shares, which are abroad, and many seamstresses who come from abroad. many seamstresses drop out because of marriage, childbirth or death.

brigitte hopes that one day she will drop out because of marriage and childbirth. brigitte hopes that heinz will get her out of here.

anything else would be the death of her, even if she stays alive.

for the time being b. has nothing but her name yet, in the course of the story brigitte will receive heinz's name, that is more important than money and property, that can procure money and property.

real life, which can give an opinion, if it's asked, real life is the life after work. for brigitte life and work is like day and night. so in this story there will be more about free time.

in this special case life is called heinz. real life is not only called heinz, it is heinz.

apart from heinz there is nothing. anything that is better than heinz is absolutely unattainable for brigitte, anything that is worse than heinz, brigitte does not want to have. brigitte fights desperately tooth and nail against going down in the world, going down in the world, that is the loss of heinz.

but brigitte also knows, that there is no going up in the world for her, there is only heinz or something worse than heinz or sewing brassières until the end of her life. sewing brassières without heinz means the end of her life right now.

it is left completely to chance, whether brigitte lives, with heinz, or escapes life and goes to waste.

there are no rules for that. fate decides brigitte's fate.

it's not what she does and is that counts, what counts is heinz and what he does and is.

brigitte and heinz have no story. brigitte and heinz only have work. heinz must become brigitte's story, he must make her a life of her own, then he must make her a child, whose future in turn will be moulded by heinz and his job.

the story of b. and h. is not something that grows, it is something that is suddenly there (flash), and is called love.

the love comes from brigitte's side. she must convince heinz that love also comes from his side. he must learn to see that for him too there can be no future without brigitte. naturally there is indeed a future for heinz, as electrician. he can have that even without brigitte. electrical wiring can be installed without b. being present at all. one can even live! and one can go bowling or play skittles without brigitte. brigitte, however, has a duty.

she must constantly make clear to heinz, that without her there is no future for him. which is a considerable effort. apart from that, strenuous measures must be taken to prevent heinz from perhaps seeing his future in someone else. more of that later.

it is a strenuous, but promising situation.

heinz wants to and will one day be a little entrepreneur with his own little enterprise. one day heinz will be placing his orders, brigitte will be ordered too. brigitte prefers to be ordered around by her own husband in his own shop, that will also in a small way be her own shop.

as long as heinz one day doesn't get to know a grammar school girl, for example, susi! as long as heinz, for heaven's sake, doesn't one day believe, that someone, who is better than brigitte ever will be, that someone like that is better for him too.

if heinz finds something better, he should leave it alone. best of all if he doesn't get to know it at all, it's safer too.

when brigitte sits at her sewing machine and stretch sews, feels foam rubber and stiff lacy borders under her fingers, the new little witch bra in the fashionable colour, then she has nightmares because of someone who does not even exist yet, but who nevertheless in the shape of something better might cross heinz's path.

brigitte doesn't even get any peace at work.

even at work she has to work.

she's not supposed to think while she's working, yet something inside her thinks uninterruptedly.

brigitte cannot make something better of her own life. something better must come from heinz's life. heinz can free brigitte from her sewing machine, brigitte cannot do it on her own.

but she cannot be certain of it, because happiness happens by chance and is not a law or the logical consequence of actions.

brigitte wants to have her future made. she cannot produce it herself.

the story of how the two of them got to know each other is not out of the ordinary. the two of them themselves are not out of the ordinary. they are simply symptomatic of everything that is not out of the ordinary.

often male and female students, which is almost the same thing, apart from their gender, meet one another too. often one can tell exciting stories about such meetings.

such people sometimes even have a long prehistory. although brigitte's prehistory is rather unfavourable for the future accumulation of wealth, she has never-theless got to know heinz, in whose hands wealth will one day accumulate.

brigitte is the illegitimate daughter of a mother, who sews the same things as brigitte, that is brassières and pantie-girdles.

heinz is the legitimate son of a van driver and his wife, who was allowed to remain at home.

despite this glaring difference b. and h. have got to know one another.

in this special case getting to know means a wanting to escape and/or a not letting slip and holding fast.

heinz has learned something, which one day will put the whole world at his feet, that is the trade of electrician.

brigitte never learned anything at all.

heinz is something, brigitte is nothing which others could not also be without any effort at all. heinz is unmistakable, and one often needs heinz too, e.g. if there's a wiring fault or one requires some love. brig-itte is replaceable and unnecessary. heinz has a future, brigitte does not even have a present.

heinz means everything to brigitte, work means nothing but burdensome misery to brigitte. a man, who loves one, is everything. a man who loves one and on top of that is someone, that is the best that brigitte can reach. work is nothing, because brigitte already has that, love is more, because one first has to find it.

brigitte has already found: heinz.

heinz often asks himself, what brigitte has to show for herself.

heinz often plays with the idea of taking someone else, someone who has something to offer, as for example, cash or suitable premises for a shop.

brigitte has a body to offer.

apart from brigitte's body many other bodies are flooding the market at the same time. the only thing that positively stands by brigitte on this path, is the cosmetics industry. and the textile industry. brigitte has breasts, thighs, legs, hips and a snatch.

others have that too, sometimes even of a better quality.

brigitte has youth, which she also has to share with others, for example with the factory and the noise in it and with the crowded bus. they gnaw at brigitte's youth.

brigitte grows ever older and ever less woman, the competition grows ever younger and ever more woman.

brigitte says to heinz i do need a man, who sticks by me, who is there for me, in return i'll stick by him too and will always be there for him.

heinz says, he doesn't give a shit about that.

it's a pity, that brigitte hates heinz so much.

today for example brigitte is kneeling on the cold floor in front of the lavatory bowl in the summer house of heinz and his parents.

this floor is colder

than love, which is hot and called heinz.

the van driver father is absent, and brigitte is helping around the house, which is the only way she can ingratiate herself, which means she enthusiastically cleans the lavatory bowl with the shit brush. five minutes ago she had said she would be happy to do that. now she's not doing it so happily any more.

she feels quite sick from all the shit which accumulates in the course of a week in a three person household.

heinz, even if he doesn't get a secretary, grammar school girl, secretary, secretary or secretary to be his wife, will nevertheless get a woman to be his wife, who is a real woman, that is knows how to handle the brush and its repulsive attendant features properly.

brigitte doesn't help at home, that would mean putting capital and labour power into a small business which was working at a loss and condemned to fail from the outset. pointless. hopeless. better for brigitte to invest where something can come of it. a completely new life.

since brigitte doesn't have much of a brain, the outcome is uncertain.

after all managers have their brain to help them when they are planning something. brigitte only had her fingers educated. nothing else. but these together with the arms attached to them could do the work of three people, if they had to. they have to. for heinz.

brigitte crawls up heinz's mummy's arse. she doesn't find anything else there either except the same shit as in the bowl, which she's just scrubbing. but one day this will lie behind me, then the future will lie before me. no, once the shit is behind me, i am already in the future. first i must work to reach a status, which enables me to be ALLOWED to have a future at all. future is a luxury. there's not much of it about.

this little episode is intended to show nothing more than that brigitte *can* work, if must be.

and it must be.

the example of paula

the example of paula, paula is from the country. until now country life has held her in check – just like her sisters erika and renate, who are married. one can already write both off, it is as if they were not in the world at all. it's different with paula, she is the youngest and still properly in the world. she is 15 years old. she is now old enough to be allowed to think about what she wants to be one day: housewife or sales assistant. sales assistant or housewife. at her age all girls, who are as old as she is, are old enough to think about what they want to be one day. secondary school is finished, the men in the village are either woodcutters or they become joiners, electricians, plumbers, bricklayers or they try to be joiners, electricians, plumbers, bricklayers and then go to the forest after all and become woodcutters. the girls become their wives. huntsman is a better job, which is imported from outside. there are no teachers and priests, the village has no church and no school. the elite profession of co-op branch manager is also imported from outside, three women and girls from the village and a girl trainee from the village always work under him. the women remain sales assistant or part-time sales assistant until their marriage, once they're married, that's the end of selling, then they are sold themselves and the next sales assistant can take her place and go on selling, the substitution is made without a hitch.

so over the years a natural cycle has come into being:

birth and starting work and getting married and leav-
ing again and getting the daughter, who is housewife
or sales assistant, usually housewife, daughter starts
work, mother kicks the bucket, daughter is married,
leaves, jumps down from the running board, herself
gets the next daughter, the co-op shop is the turn-
table of the natural cycle of nature, the seasons and
human life in all its many forms of expression are
reflected in its fruit and veg. in its single display
window are reflected the attentive faces of its sales
assistants, who have come together here to wait for
marriage and for life. but marriage always comes
alone, without life. hardly ever does a married
woman work in the shop, unless her husband is
unemployed or seriously injured. he's always an
alcoholic.
as a woodcutter he has a hard and dangerous job,
from which many a man has often not come back
again. that is why they enjoy their life tremendously,
as long as they are young, from 13 upwards no girl
is safe from them, the universal race begins, and wild
oats are sown and young men lock horns, a process
which echoes through the whole village. the process
echoes down the valley.
at the end of their youth the young men take a hard-
working thrifty woman into the house. end of youth.
beginning of old age.
for the woman end of life and start of having
children. while the men mature nicely and begin to
age and take to drink, it will keep them strong and
free of cancer, the death throes of their wives often
last for years and years, and often so long that they
can even be present at their daughters' death throes.
the women begin to hate their daughters and want

to have them die as quickly as possible just as they once died, so: so they must get a man.

sometimes a daughter does not want to die as quickly as she should, but prefers to remain a sales assistant for one or two years and live! yes live! in rare cases she would even like to become sales assistant in the county town, where there are other professions such as priest, teacher, factory worker, plumber, joiner, locksmith, but also watchmaker, baker, butcher! and pork butcher! and many more. many more promises of life in a more beautiful future.

yet it is far from easy, to be able to grab hold of a man with a more beautiful future. the better jobs also have something better to offer, that's why they demand right away that one does it, nevertheless one must not do it, because otherwise the better job wants something even better right away, and that's that. a forestry lad sometimes waits, a better job never waits. hardly anyone has ever come back, except to visit and with a bastard without a dada.

the few others also sometimes come home to visit, to show mother and dada the children, how well they're doing, and the husband is good and hands over all the money and only drinks a little, and the kitchen is all new and the vacuum cleaner is new and the curtains are new and the corner table ditto and the tv is new and the new settee is new and the new cooker is admittedly used but as new, and the floor tiles are admittedly worn but scrubbed like new. and the daughter is still as new, but will soon be a sales assistant and rapidly age and become used. but why should the daughter not become used up, if the mother has been used up too? the daughter must be used soon, she really needs it urgently, and so let's have the new and the better, that is priest, teacher, factory worker, plumber, joiner, locksmith, watchmaker, butcher! and pork butcher! and many more, etc and all of them uninterruptedly need women and make use of them too, but they themselves by no means want to buy an already used woman for further use. no. that makes things difficult. because where does one get unused women from, if women are constantly being used? there is no prostitution, but there are a lot of illegitimate children, she, she should not have done it, but she did do it, and it was made for her, it was really given to her, and now she's left standing and has to do the work herself, even the work a husband usually does, and the child stays with the hate-of-mother-and-children-filled granny. used women are rarely taken, and then only by the first user. then they have to hear for the rest of their life: if i hadn't taken you, no one else would have taken you, and where would you get the money for the child, but i took you at the last moment after all, and now you can take money from me, after i've taken the money for drink first, and then i can take you in return without any problem as often as i like, but i'll make sure, that nobody takes and uses our daughter unlawfully, so that she doesn't turn into someone like her mother, who let herself be taken BEFORE.

she must wait, till someone takes her, but afterwards, and then let herself be taken, but only afterwards. because if, like you, she lets herself be taken before, then she can count herself lucky afterwards, if anyone takes her at all. and our daughter can be glad, that she's got a dada like me.

terrible, this slow dying. and the husbands and the

wives die away together, the husband does get a bit of variety, he watches over his wife like a watchdog outside, he watches over her as she dies. and from the inside the wife watches over the husband, the female summer visitors, her daughter and the house-keeping money, which must not be boozed away. and from outside the man watches over his wife, the male summer visitors, his daughter and the housekeeping money, so that he can divert some for his boozing. and so they die in mutual dependence. and the daughter can hardly wait, to be allowed to die at last also, and the parents are already going shopping for the daughter's death: sheets and towels and dish cloths and a used refrigerator. then at least she'll stay dead but fresh.

and what will become of paula? sales assistant or housewife? with everything else, let's not forget paula! which this is about. what will become of paula? die later or sooner? or not start out on life at all? die right away? not be able to wait, and then it's too late, and the child is there and the mother dies right away instead of after the wedding? NO! because paula wants to learn dressmaking. that's never happened before in the village, that a girl wants to LEARN something. it's bound to go wrong. her mother asks: paula, don't you want to be a sales assistant after all, where you can get to know someone or a housewife once you've got to know someone?

her mother says: paula, you MUST become a sales assistant or a housewife. paula replies: mother, there isn't a vacancy as trainee sales assistant available just now. her mother says: then stay at home, paula, and become a housewife and help me with the housework and with the animals and wait upon your dada as i wait upon him and also wait upon your brother, when he comes from the wood, why should you be better off than me, I was never better off than my mother, who was a housewife, because in those days there weren't any sales assistants here yet, and my dada would have beaten me to death if there had been any.

and he said, i have to stay at home and help momma and attend to him, when he comes from work and fetch the beer from the innkeeper, that takes eight minutes there and back, and if it takes longer, then i'll break your back. and why should you, my daughter, be better off than me? just stay at home and help me, when your dada and your brother gerald come home. and perhaps one day we, i and your dada and your brother gerald will really break your back. HELLO!

however paula says, but mother i don't want to, i want to learn dressmaking. and when i've finished learning to be a dressmaker, i want to have something of my life, drive to italy and go to the cinema with the money i've earned myself, and after i've had something of life, i want to drive to italy once more, for the last time and, with the money i've earned, go to the cinema once again, for the very last time, and then i want to look for a decent man, or a less decent man, such as one sees in the cinema more and more often now, and then i want to marry and have children. and all together and love them at the same time, yes love! and there will be two, a boy and a girl, and then i would like to take the pill as well, so that there are only two, a boy and a girl, and everything's always clean and neat. and then only have to sew for the children and myself, and a detached house, built ourselves with a hardworking husband.

and for the children and myself i'll sew everything, that will save a lot of money, then i'll no longer have to sew for strangers, he won't allow that, no. momma, please, i want to learn dressmaking.

momma says, that she will tell dada and gerald. she at most went to the cinema three times in her life, and she didn't like it and it didn't interest her, and she was glad when she was home again. i haven't been to italy at all, never, and the tv is much more interesting, one sees the whole world, without wanting or having to be in it the whole time. when my dada was still alive, i slaved for him, and then i went on slaving for your dada and for gerald, and now that you're old enough to slave with me, you suddenly don't want to any more but learn the clean trade of dressmaking instead. why and for what have i slaved all my life, if not for dada and gerald, and now when you could at last slave with me, you don't want to. you can put it out of your head! before dada and gerald put it out of your head for you. i'll tell dada and gerald right now. right now!

dada and gerald take the view, that paula can't be allowed to shirk things by doing light clean dressmaking, when they themselves do heavy dirty woodcutting. she better not believe, that she can escape dada's hate, with a clean job, when dada after all had to marry mother because of her, well, not because of her but because of her eldest sister, who is already married now and unassailable. since we already hated your momma, because she was allowed to do clean housework, while we have to do the dirty heavy work, so we've time and again beaten your momma half

dead when we were drunk, so we've thrown our dirty
boots in your momma's face and our dirty trousers
onto the bench, our dirty work trousers onto the then
new upholstered bench, so we also want frequently to
throw our dirty boots in your face too and our dirty
trousers onto the bench, which you then must clear
up. have we forgotten our honest clean hatred of
you both even for a moment? no. you see! except for
the moment of a birthday, of a christmas eve or of
a serious accident, and you want to learn dressmaking!

but paula goes on looking at the better world, wherever she can grab hold of it, no matter where, in the
cinema or with a summer visitor. but it is always only
the better life of others, never her own.

she also says sometimes: you could use the apprenticeship allowance, and after all one has to train as a
sales assistant too. and my wedding dress, just think,
then i can sew my wedding dress myself!!! and i can
sew something for momma too, and for my aunt and
for my granny and everybody, everybody. and that
saves money again, and while i'm doing it, i'll often
see clean people, and then i too will be one of the
clean people, because i'll sew myself new clothes too,
which a better man might like.

and everybody will say i'm clean, and perhaps then
i'll even be married by a joiner, bricklayer, plumber,
butcher! or pork butcher!

and all the time paula looks on the better life as
something that can belong to her some day too,
although it is not made for her.

and because she isn't worth all the trouble anyway,
and because dada wants to be left in peace in the
evening, and because he can't knock her to the

ground, much as he would like to, because he is simply too tired, to be able to risk a second outburst of rage, and because he can't kill her, much as he would like to, and because basically he doesn't give two hoots, and because paula has promised a thousand things, among them, that she will help her mother in the sty in the evening, and because money is money, paula is at last allowed to learn dressmaking.

and from this moment on paula sees the better life with quite different eyes, as something, that one can perhaps even get, although first one has to take up the hem and take in the waist.

so paula's apprenticeship begins in the bad old life, it's supposed to come to an end in the better new one. let's hope it doesn't end, even before it has properly begun.

and let's hope the better life doesn't already belong to someone else, someone perhaps who might no longer like a narrower waist and a shorter skirt.

what is it, that shines so bright?

what is it, that's shining there as bright as ripe polished chestnuts, heinz asks himself one day on the way to work. it is brigitte's hair, that has been newly tinted. one must only take care not to leave it on too long.

heinz thought, that it's ripe polished chestnuts, shining so brightly there, but now he sees that it's brigitte's hair, that shines so brightly there. he is astonished that fate has struck a blow.

i love you, says brigitte. her hair gleams in the sun

like ripe chestnuts, which have been polished too. i love you so much. that is the feeling of love this inescapable feeling. i feel, as if i had always known you, even in my childhood, which is long past. brigitte looks up at heinz.

heinz too is immediately gripped by the feeling. apart from that he is gripped by a sensuality, of whose existence he has already heard.

it is new and terrifying at once.

heinz wants to be an electrician. if one learns something, then afterwards one is more than one was before. apart from that one is then more than all those, who have learned nothing.

something is happening to the two of us here, says brigitte, which is newer and more terrifying than everything which has happened to us until now, newer and more terrifying even than the factory accident last year, in which a hand was lost: love. because i know now, that i love you and am glad, that i know. for me there is no other man but you, heinz, and there will never be another. or do you see another man here? heinz does not see another man, and the feeling of sensuality grows even stronger. these lips are literally casting their spell on me, thinks heinz. they tempt, and they promise something. what? heinz thinks. now he has it: sensuality.

i love you so much, says brigitte, her hair gleams like ripe chestnuts in the sun. her full lips are slightly open, as if they were tempting or at least promising. what? i love you so much, that it hurts, it hurts soulfully in my soul and bodily in my body. i want you always to stay with me, and never leave me. after the wedding i want to stay entirely at home and be there only for you and our common child.

what is my work in the factory compared to this feeling of love? nothing! it disappears and only the feeling of love is here.

heinz wants to buy himself a new fashionable pair of trousers. now that he is loved, a modern pair of trousers is much more important even than before. unfortunately all the wages of his final year as an apprentice are swallowed up in the discotheques at the weekends. there too there is sensuality, but less than here with brigitte, where it is immediately relevant.

i need you and i love you, says brigitte. her hair shines in the sun like ripe polished chestnuts, love is the feeling that one person needs the other. i need you, says brigitte, so that i no longer have to go to the factory, because really i don't need the factory at all. what i need is you and being near you. i love you and i need you.

hopefully this love is also physical, hopes heinz. a man has to take everything he can get. also he must one day have a beautiful home, which he has to save up for beforehand, also he must one day have children, but beforehand he must have had something of life. work isn't everything, because love is everything. could that be physical love, asks heinz.

yes, heinz, it's love, says brigitte. her hair shimmers in the sun like ripe polished chestnuts. suddenly it has come to us, overnight, heinz, who would have thought? you will take care of me and repay and reward me for my love, won't you, heinz?

because i love you so much.

heinz keeps one eye on his professional advancement and on courses which are perhaps to be attended. brigitte keeps an eye on love, which is like a serious illness, and brigitte keeps the other eye on her future home and its furnishings. brigitte has heard that it's real, if it's like an illness, brigitte loves heinz really and truly.

never leave me, heinz!

making a great sacrifice heinz's parents buy the modern pair of trousers for heinz. but in return they don't want anything silly going on between girls and heinz. they say, he can ruin his whole professional future with things like that. hasn't father slogged away enough all his life? one ruined life in the family really is enough.

for heinz, who wants to achieve something, the future is important. heinz, who until now has not achieved anything in life, says: life does not consist only of work. you haven't learned anything and not achieved anything in life yet, that's why you can't know that, says his father, who hasn't achieved or learned anything either and is already old.

i love you, says brigitte. who doesn't want to lose heinz. what one has, one wants to keep, possibly one can even get more than one has. perhaps a shop of one's own. she can work hard too, which she is used to.

i love you, says brigitte. at last one no longer has to ask, whether this is love, because she is sure of it. heinz and brigitte are frightened by the magnitude of this feeling. brigitte is more frightened than heinz, because feelings are more feminine.

a job is more manly. heinz doesn't enjoy it much, nevertheless he wants to get on, where he gets to doesn't matter. admittedly heinz enjoys love more, nevertheless he has to be careful, so that he is not impeded professionally by it. the fashionable items of clothing, which heinz will be able to buy himself from his wages, will certainly make him happy, the fashionable items of clothing, which he will have to buy his wife, will certainly make him much less happy. therefore: watch out!

love hurts brigitte. she is waiting for a phone call from heinz. why doesn't it ring? it hurts so much to wait. it hurts because brigitte is longing for heinz. brigitte says, that heinz is her whole world. brigitte's world is therefore small. life seems meaningless without him, even with him life doesn't seem to be very meaningful, it just looks more meaningful, at any rate more meaningful than her work in the brassière factory.

come back, heinz! i love you, and i need you.

heinz needs a secure livelihood. something inside him says: strive to get on, that's what his more experienced parents say too, who have never been outside the country.

don't leave me alone ever again, begs brigitte, my life is meaningless without your life.

brigitte must make sure, that she gets a man, who doesn't go to the inn. she must make sure, that she gets a nice house. she must make sure, that she gets children. she must make sure, that she gets nice furniture. then she must make sure, that she doesn't have to go to work any more. then before that she must make sure, that the car is paid off. then she must make sure, that she can afford a nice holiday every year. then, however, she must make sure, that she doesn't have to turn a blind eye.

you only live once, says brigitte's mother, for whom this one time is already too much and too often, because she doesn't have a husband.

brigitte's one life is filled, however, because it is full of heinz. her hair gleams in the sun like polished chestnuts. brigitte is quite overwhelmed by this life, which, thanks to heinz, is almost a size too big for her. brigitte is not overwhelmed by her work, because it is monotonous. heinz, in contrast to her work, is overwhelming.

heinz has still to get somewhere in life, before he can even think of a family. brigitte wants to get heinz, who will then get somewhere for her, because he has a future. heinz's future is the electrical trade, in which he is active. brigitte's future lies in heinz. good craftsmen are a scarce commodity.

my god, how i love you, says brigitte to heinz.

i can feel it too this this feeling, replies heinz. his father feels the discs in his back, because he is a van driver, which soon he will have been, if his discs don't behave themselves. the van driver believes, that brigitte is nothing and has nothing. he believes, that heinz will be something and already has something now: that is, talent, tenacity and a capacity for hard work. do not disappoint your father, heinz! he believes that you can and must demand high standards.

best of all, if heinz looks for a woman with money, so that he can soon set up on his own and get his own shop. pretty faces like brigitte's often deceive, in them lies professional downfall. his parents want the best for heinz. brigitte is certainly not that: the BEST.

i love you so much, says brigitte. my gleaming hair supports my love. what also supports my love: your job, which has a future. what supports my love apart from that: i myself, who have nothing at all.

heinz's parents want heinz to look out for the genuine article, which brigitte's hair is not. it's dyed. heinz is still far too young to know the genuine article when he sees it. his parents are responsible for the genuine article, because they've been dealing with it all their lives. his father feels, that his discs must be very very genuine. heinz can demand high standards, which after all is why he learned his trade.

brigitte very much loves the genuine article too. heinz, the genuine man, for example, then genuine carpets, genuine living room suites and a genuine little drinks cabinet.

heinz still wants to have something of his life. heinz can still have something of his life, as long as he stays with his parents and saves money. apart from that he's still too young to tie himself down. brigitte, whose hair is gleaming again today, so much that it hurts the eyes, loves heinz so much, that something in her would break, if heinz throws her away. i love you, she says in the manner of her favourites from film, radio, television and records. i don't know if it's enough for a whole life, says heinz, a man wants to enjoy many women, a man is different.

but that's exactly why i love you, because you are a man, says brigitte. you are a man, who is learning a trade, i am a woman, who has not learned a trade. your trade must do for both of us. and it will do that easily, because it's such a beautiful trade. you must never leave me, otherwise i would die, says brigitte.

no one dies as easily as that, says heinz. you would just have to fall back on someone, who earns less, than i shall earn one day.

but that's exactly why i love you, because you earn more than someone, who earns less.

apart from that brigitte loves heinz, because this feeling is inside her, which she can't fight. full stop.
her hair is like polished sweet chestnuts.
i'll sleep on it says heinz. that's how it's done in the modern business world, which i know all about.
i love you so much, replies brigitte. tomorrow is already the future, and that i don't have.
you don't have me either, says heinz.
so i wouldn't like to be in your shoes.

and on goes paula the bad example

always alternating with the good example, brigitte, paula, the bad example, trails along.
when it is still almost night, paula trails into the neighbouring town, which is almost a city, where one can therefore also learn a trade, which can possibly change a whole life: dressmaking.
in the neighbouring town one also learns superfluous things, which could lead one astray: cinema and café going.
paula has already often been warned against both.
it is so nice to sit down in a café.
it is as if one had come into the world for something beautiful. and yet one has come into the world for something unpleasant: for a false life, which is called housework, and which sticks to one, if one touches it by mistake.
at home paula works for her family, whom she has to thank for this false life.
is anybody surprised that there is a longing in paula?
in the bus apart from her a lot of children are going

to school and a lot of women to the butcher! pork butcher! or cemetery.

no man under 70 is going by bus, unless he is sick. but bus journeys are not allowed when one is sick. every kind of pleasure is immediately reported to the foreman. that's why every man under 70 is illegally on the bus. the legal men under 70 drive by jeep up into the high forest.

the housewives on the bus declare to paula in chorus, that paula is one of them.

the housewives on the bus declare emphatically, that she's nothing better.

but above everything is love, which is best of all, replies paula. paula is better, because she will have love inside, when the right moment comes. first of all paula is better because of dressmaking, subsequently she will be ennobled by love. love will take the place of dressmaking. i am already so glad.

paula holds on tight to her little leather bag, which is something better than the plastic carrier bags of the others of her species. the other women hold on tight to their knowledge about men, which paula doesn't have yet.

men can be pigs, but also the opposite. what is the opposite of a pig?

but the men work hard all week. saturday is the great day of subjugation. then the village trembles from all the knee, back and shoulder throws.

paula trembles, when she hears that, with her everything will be quite different. better.

afterwards one can lick one's wounds over coffee and watch television. yes, television! the afternoon programmes. in front of an amusing cartoon film, which one only understands half of, because it happens so fast, every pain in one's abdomen forgets to stab.

if a pain in the abdomen does nevertheless stick out its head like a worm out of the apple, then it's too late, the old proverb says, women are born to suffer, men are born to work: someone has got stuck into the body of the other and is laying waste inside it, living, feeding off it, that is called symbiosis.

apart from that the women on the bus have the advantage over paula of the knowledge of the beneficial pain of getting children. the start is large, but it can be made up. many conversations echo through the stale air, which deal with pain in general, the unhealthy pain of carrying and fetching, of being operated on, of rheumatism, of hernias, backache, cataracts or cancer. then one discusses the beneficial pains of bearing children, which each time make a woman stronger. which is immediately and without a break followed by the great joy of having a child, which draws after it the enormous joy of lying in.

paula, the victim of the business, is learning dressmaking. she can already manage an apron. it takes time, but she can do it. paula enjoys the activity of handling cloth. often however, just when paula has to sew a particularly complicated seam, love sticks its ugly head in the way. since paula is learning more and more about love in her breaks, mostly from comic books, paula knows even while she's working, what happens between men and women. at any rate new and different from how she's ever heard it before. what paula has ever heard before, she got from her family and her girlfriends. but what can one expect from such subhuman creatures! paula would be crazy to show any solidarity with the women in her family, with these poor doormats! paula would rather show solidarity with her best friend, the singer and actress uschi glas, or with her second-best friend, the good-looking blonde wife of this good-looking dark pop singer (black hair).

in the breaks paula soaks up love, when she's working she pukes it all up again. above all, that it has to be clean but sensual. that's a thorn in paula's flesh. how could love ever prosper and grow in her unsensual and unclean surroundings, yes how?

what is the result, if one imagines something, which does not exist in the reality of the person who is doing the imagining? right: dreams result from this cruel constellation.

like all women paula dreams of love.

all women, including paula, dream of love.

many of her former schoolfriends, many of her present workmates, dream about it as well, except each one of them firmly believes, that only she will find it.

while selling as a sales assistant, the star job, love has the opportunity and the chance to come walking in a hundred times a day. but it's always only house-wives with children who come in, never love. the housewives who have come in, who have already had love once, a long time ago, feel sorry for and despise the sales assistants, because they have to sell and cannot enjoy the most beautiful results of love, that is, the children and the housekeeping money, which comes from the husband and for the most part returns there again.

the protected women despise the unprotected ones. and the sales assistants hate the housewives in return, because the latter have got everything behind them, while they still have to face a tough competitive struggle and instead of varnished furniture still have to buy nylon stockings, pullovers and mini skirts – as investments.

yes, it all costs money.

there is a universal hating in the place, which is spreading more and more, which infects everything, which affects everyone, the women discover nothing in common, only differences. those, who have got something better because of their physical advantages, want to hold on to it and hide it from others, the others want to take it away from them or have something even better. there is a hating and a despising.

the foundation stone is already laid at school. that paula at all thinks of comparing love with flowers, buds, grasses and foliage, is a result of her school days.

that paula connects love with sensuality, is a result of the magazines, which she likes to read. paula has already heard, but not quite understood, the word sensuality.

nobody likes to say, that love only has something to do with work. paula even knows in her sleep, how to feed a baby and put on a nappy. but paula does not know, how to prevent conception.

but paula knows in her sleep, what really matters, that is feelings alone.

paula is waiting to be chosen, which is what really matters. what matters is to be chosen by the right man.

paula herself has never learned to choose and to decide. paula experiences everything in the passive voice, not in the active voice. the utmost that paula experiences, is that she could say no. but one should not say no too often, because otherwise one has said no once too often, and in future happiness passes by and doesn't ring again.

paula sometimes goes onto the dance floor, if there's a party. sometimes paula is led away into the woods again by a drunk dance floor visitor, which no one must see, because that would immediately cause her market value to go through the floor.

in the woods then paula is grabbed by her breasts or at worst between the legs or by the arse.

paula has been taught to assess who is grabbing her there between the legs. is it someone with or without a future.

is it someone with a future or a work horse?

if it is a work horse, then he cannot become paula's fate. paula's brain has learned to work like a computer in such cases. here's the printout: married, two children.

now follows the shoving away, cursing, shrieking, sometimes there follows the swaying and falling over of the alcoholic and seducer.

sometimes there follows the falling over, giving up and sleeping it off.

sometimes the said person also turns brutal and rough.

it is not enough therefore, simply to surrender oneself brainlessly to love, when it knocks at the door, one must also calculate because of later life, which does sometimes follow.

one must calculate because of the future, which is still before one.

the future, that is always someone else, it always comes from the other person. the future strikes one like hail stones. love, if at all, like a thunderstorm. at worst not at all. dressmaking one has to do oneself. dressmaking one has to do oneself.

paula immediately starts to think, therefore to programme, when someone touches her. then often quite unprogrammed nausea rises up. out with it! but it's swallowed down right away. let's just hope that in her zeal, paula doesn't ever inadvertently swallow down love along with it!

paula learns early to regard her body and what happens to it, as something that happens to someone else. a second body as it were, a second paula.

all the material from paula's dreams, all the tenderness happens with paula's first body, the thrashings which come from dada, happen to her second body, her mother, who has never learned to acquire a second body, has to absorb everything with her first body, that's why it's already so worn out and tired.

one just has to know how to look out for oneself. one must be able to look out for oneself somehow! if one cannot take anything for oneself, apart from work, if one is always only taken, then one just has to look out for oneself.

when the women talk about their husbands, then they only say: mine. MINE. nothing else, not my man, only mine. perhaps to a stranger one says: my husband. to someone from here one says: mine. paula observes the victor's smile, when momma or her sisters say: mine. the only occasion, on which the vanquished have a victor's smile in the corner of their mouths.

she also wants one day to say to someone: mine. about her dressmaking paula never says: my work. about her work paula never says: mine. not even inwardly. work, that is something, which is detached from a person, work after all is more like a duty and so it happens to the second body. love, that's pleasure, relaxation, and so it happens to the first body.

one suffers work, even if one enjoys doing it. paula despite all her love of dressmaking, has learned that work is something burdensome, which only keeps love away, does not bring it close.

only a cement mixer can sort things out in paula's skull. amidst all that physical love and all that spiritual love of film actresses, pop singers and tv stars.

paula only records, she doesn't digest. like a sponge which is never squeezed out. a sponge which is saturated, from which any excess only runs off more by chance. how on earth can paula learn anything?

through suffering of course.

which makes one wise.

brigitte also is repelled by heinz
brigitte is also repelled by heinz

brigitte also is repelled by heinz and his plump white electrician's body, which is also called heinz. despite that she is also happy again, so happy, dead happy, that she has him, because he is her future.

do you have a future too? form a complete sentence: my future is called eddy. and brigitte must produce all her feelings by herself, with the aid of her physical strength alone. without technical aid.

no wonder it's too much for her.

heinz utilises his physical strength, to provide himself with a profession.

heinz also has brains, which is a help too.

brigitte doesn't trust her physical strength to be able to provide a profession for herself, brigitte just manages to produce love.

one day heinz's married sister with her baby and her small child come to visit. brigitte stumbles around, heavily laden with cups, cake plates and the cakes that go with them. heinz's mother would like to hide brigitte, perhaps in the hydrangea bed?! because the latter only sews on the brassière production line, always at least forty items, that is the piecework target. brigitte wants to belong at all costs, she wants to anchor her future in the present so firmly, that no one can tear it away from her again.

heinz's mother, however, by nature good-humoured, sees heinz's future only in heinz alone, in heinz and his presumptive detached house, that he will be able to provide for mummy, daddy and not least himself with his small businessman's money. wants to and will. heinz's mother already sees it all before her like a mirage, a patient future, which has already borne much, even before it exists at all, a future on whose back the little house spreads out. children, won't that be nice! nowhere does mother see a little place for brigitte, not even in the kitchen, brigitte's little place is the line, the line and nothing but the line, loaded down with lacy brassière borders, foam rubber and stretch fabric, brigitte's little house is sewing, which she learned on the job.

first of all a shop of his own must be established, which swallows up a lot of money, which swallows up a lot of the van driver savings. once, many years ago, heinz's mother, before she became a van driver's wife, even before she became a future businessman's mother, had been nothing and a nobody. so she knows this condition inside out.

she herself is out of it in any case and old. father is still inside, he became a van driver. his discs are admittedly irrevocably worn out, but despite that daddy can still lift his son onto his shoulders and carry him, lift him into the saddle, into the world of business.

heinz's mummy shoves brigitte under the coffee table, stuffs her into the china cupboard. brigitte has to hand over everything she's carrying, the cake, the whipped cream, the little sugar bowl and the coffee pot. brigitte is not allowed to help.

mummy herself and in person, the mother person, carries all this in helped by her married daughter and mother of her grandchildren. over the coffee the women talk about the household, the appliances that go with it, the earners of the household money and the children.

over coffee the men talk about football, football, work, money and about football.

the men don't talk about the women, because they are here, whether they talk about them or not.

heinz's married sister describes, what it's like, to feel a small breathing child's body beside one, a helpless little something, which was in the process of becoming for a while and now at last has become a life, this infant, as small as he is, he has nevertheless at last made her a woman.

brigitte would like to exchange experiences too, but she has nothing to offer in exchange.

heinz's sister explains, how it's done, to present the dear husband with a child. now at last he has the little child.

the presentation has been accomplished.

it was an inspiring event.

brigitte has secretly crawled out of the china cupboard in which she was looking for china, although it was no business of hers, and has joined the company, even though she has no business being there. she nods loudly at heinz's sister's every sentence. she offers as an example, that now it's still nice to buy herself pretty clothes for heinz, to please him, but how really nice it will one day be, when she no longer has to buy pretty clothes for herself, because she will have become a mother. when the presentation of one or more children has been accomplished. that will be the result of her great love, the little child.

angry objection by the others, who have only just reported so positively on children and their discharge.

brigitte explains, that such a tiny being would make her a mother a mother a mother, that heinz doesn't know what to do with babies, because he is a man, that she knows very well what to do with babies, because she is a woman. heinz will learn to love the baby later, brigitte will be able to love it right away and on the spot.

heinz is still rather more in favour of pleasure and profit.

heinz's mother is still rather more in favour of an enlargement of the little house, so that at last there will be a resting place for the ruined discs. heinz is secretly in favour of the old people's home, after the van driver savings have been set in concrete. first of all one has to turn the savings of a transient life into durable concrete. brigitte is in every case in favour of heinz and in favour of what heinz is in favour of.

naturally they'll never get anywhere they want to get to, if they go on like that.

in the garden there are so many green fruit-laden branches they could reach. in the garden there are also flowers for cutting, which one should pick, as long as they are blooming.

heinz's father is an authority on such questions.

in reality brigitte is repelled by infants. in reality she would love to snap the delicate little fingers, and stud the helpless little toes with bamboo splinters and stuff a dirty rag into the gob of the newly arrived number one instead of the beloved pacifier, so that for once there really would be something to scream about.

if those present only knew what a transformation into a monster has occurred inside brigitte.

meanwhile however the baby of heinz's sister pees vigorously on brigitte's head as well, right onto the new hair tint, into the new long-lasting perm, which causes renewed laughter. brigitte, who is just picking up a little silver plated spoon, stands up, and her fingers automatically clench like birds' claws, these are fingers which usually have to fight for everything.

brigitte cannot bear such humiliation in front of everyone at all. a person like brigitte can often even break because of little things.

there are many big things, which have already happened, and haven't broken brigitte either.

everyone laughs at baby's joke, even heinz's father, who has nothing much to laugh at any more. even his discs laugh along today. the child laughs loudest. even the love, which is at home in the small world laughs along. brigitte's world is the small world of love. she dries baby off, well done baby!

heinz's mother shoos brigitte back into the kitchen.

that's all we need, that the unskilled worker wants to have a child like that too, and perhaps even by our lad heinz!

the old people's home waves threateningly from afar, it's never yet been mentioned, but is present none the less.

it will put in an appearance at the right moment.

we shall make our own future, says heinz's mother.

but then it belongs to us, and only to us. let her go and make her own. heinz, our son, is making our future. ours, his, but not any other future.

why does brigitte want so much, yes, just about all of it really, that is, our boy?

why is brigitte simply not content with what she's got, that is, nothing?

others don't have anything either, but are content.

if one is content, then something even comes of nothing.

why can't brigitte be content with the nothing that she has?

baby tramples on brigitte's woolly hair.

baby pokes his baby fingers in brigitte's eyes, ears and nose.

everyone laughs heartily, even the morose father and ambitious heinz.

hope laughs too, although there is one hope less again.

the future cannot laugh, because it has not arrived yet.

the present doesn't laugh, because it's too weighed down for that.

brigitte's work doesn't laugh at all, because it's too far away.

because today is a holiday for everyone!

brigitte puts a good face on things and laughs along heartily. then she goes to wash herself.

her teeth grind very loudly with hate.

even the most durable love must fall silent at so much hate.

it draws back in fright.

from this moment heinz has become a serious duty and not love.

from pleasure to work.

brigitte knows more about work anyway.

heinz's sister laughs loudest, because she is safe. nothing more can happen to her, she's made it.

heinz's mother's laugh is somewhat forced, because brigitte has still not fled the field before heinz's better future.

because brigitte is still in the game and evidently intends to stay in it.

fortune smiles on all of them.

yet one day

yet one day what makes a human being fully human happened to paula too. we've waited long enough for it. on that day it suddenly seemed to her as if until then she had not really lived.

because: until then life had only been work, the house, the household, the girlfriends, work, the work at home and the work at the dressmaker's (only recently!), a false or incomplete life therefore. but

now this is wiped out, and love is there, and it has come at last, and now at last paula is a human being. work, the house, the household, the girlfriends, work, the work at home and the work at the dressmaker's are admittedly still there, they don't go away by themselves from one day to the next, but apart from that love is here too now, hurrah, the most imp. thing in human life and now also the most imp. thing in paula's life.
paula has come to a very firm decision on that.
she also wants to do everything properly.
and she MUST do everything properly, otherwise love will just be gone again, or it will be driven out by work, the house, the household, the girlfriends, work, the work at home and the work at the dress-maker's, so that it would fall hopelessly behind.
at least she'll still have the household.
because erich is the handsomest in the village. admittedly erich is an only child with three other siblings each with a different dada, which makes for a poor starting position, as one knows, but he is handsome.
as handsome as a picture with his black hair and blue eyes, just the one to fall in love with.
erich is also desired by others.
even if it is not so important for a man to be good-looking, whereas it is very important for a woman, it is nevertheless nice if a man is good-looking. erich also has an interesting job: he is a woodcutter. despite that erich doesn't enjoy his work, although it is very interesting, but the forest nevertheless needs people, therefore: to the forest, erich, right after secondary school! erich likes to be useful.
suddenly paula doesn't give a hoot about any of that.

all that matters is that love has come at last, and that it hasn't come to an ugly, worn out, drunken, exhausted, vulgar, common woodcutter and her, but to a handsome, worn out, drunken, strong, vulgar, common woodcutter and her. that makes the whole thing special. love in itself is already something special, certainly, but how special must it be, when circumstances choose erich and paula for love. erich and paula are one in a thousand, perhaps even one in a million!

paula, who has been waiting for this day for many years, perhaps for ever, asks love in right away and pours out a cup of good coffee and puts a large piece of cake beside it. otherwise erich, who was the epitome of manliness, even before love had struck, and who is now the epitome of manliness altogether for her, because the other men she knows, could not be epitomes of anything, at most of alcohol or beating or the smell of resin, otherwise erich will never come into her little kitchen. but today erich is coming, the epitome of the manly man, the epitome of alcoholism, of beating which he has received since earliest childhood from momma, grandmomma, his stepfather and his workmates in the forest, today erich is coming into the kitchen. as small, shabby and the worse for wear as it is, it is so clean that one could eat off the floor. erich has a message to pass on, an extremely important piece of information to do with the outing tomorrow. the organiser of the trip has sent him. he has difficulties speaking, just as he has with everything else.

take a seat, erich. erich says: as small, shabby and the worse for wear as your kitchen is, it is nevertheless clean as a new pin. you must be a very great help to your momma, paula. well done!

paula glows at this praise like a whitsun ox in all its glory.

at this point in time paula is exactly 15, erich on the other hand 23 years old. that is important, because before everything was different and afterwards too everything will be quite different. let us stop this moment in time! at this point in time, it is not yet time for paula to begin thinking about marriage. if paula were to think about marriage, her dada would scrape the flesh from her bones. if erich were to think about marriage, his grandmomma, his momma and his stepfather would immediately try to beat that idea out of him. AND WHO WILL DO YOUR WORK? who will mow and feed the animals and spread manure? who? and who will fetch the pig swill? who???

and his momma who was always in service away from home, from her fourteenth year, that is one year younger than paula is now, who was always in service, in the county town, in fact in several county towns county towns, which has brought her four children, each by a different daddy, a hip problem, chronic bronchial catarrh, an unbelievably ugly shrivelled up face, a round back from washing floors, two gold teeth! and her final man, her only legally married husband, a retired railway official, who is the very one she doesn't have a child by, and who for that reason keeps even more of an eye on her, but more of that later, so his momma, who is now in service at home, round the clock, whose back is getting even more crooked from washing floors, whose hip problem and bronchial catarrh is getting even worse than it ever was, but who is happy to slave away, it's for the upright pensioner and husband who didn't need to marry her with her four children, and who would never have married her either, if he were not a nasty asthmatic in need of care, this momma says at last, after an interval of significant silence: you can't have anything at all, but if you can have something, then something BETTER, erich. go out into the wide world, as i once went out, which has helped me on a lot in life, that is, to an official with a pension, even if the path was sometimes steep and led over false, bad men and their false, bad seed inside me, so get right away from here, to where things are better, outwardly you look better anyway, your father was an italian after all, so you'll easily get a wife with dough, the way you look with your black, foreign hair, you look better than the local boys with their local sandy to dirty brown hair, the way you look you'll easily get a wife with money, one of those one hears, reads and sees so much of.

and that will benefit us then too. you better watch out, if it doesn't benefit us too.

so don't take any girl at all, but if you must take someone, then don't take anyone from here, take one from somewhere else, where things are better. but you are a man after all, you can look after yourself. you are a man after all. just look out, that you don't give anyone a bastard, because under certain circumstances that will cost you a fortune and your future, erich. and if you must, then at least give it to someone, who's got dough, a summer visitor, for example. so go away from home, perhaps even abroad, which exists as well, and of which i've seen so many beautiful colour photographs.

and make sure you don't disturb dada's afternoon nap, which he needs with his bad asthma, otherwise he'll get a fit of choking again, and we've had it. and make sure for my sake that you don't disturb dada's afternoon nap, because he was on the railways, and that's more than anyone else here can say for themselves, otherwise he'll die while he's in my hands. i'll take his coffee in to him right now, then it'll already be there when he wakes up.

and just make sure for my sake that you don't disturb dada's afternoon nap, which he needs for his bad bronchial asthma, because he was on the railways, because he is too weak, still to be able to beat you, and i'm too weak to do it too.

it's true you're good-looking and dark erich, but you're not god's gift. nevertheless afterwards take a look at the photos of other countries again, it won't do you any harm, even if you don't understand them. as good-looking and dark as you are, erich, you haven't got much in your head.

after that erich puts on the new pullover from the mail order catalogue, the new blue jeans from the mail order catalogue and finally the most beautiful thing of all from the mail order catalogue: the patterned pure wool woollen jacket. erich, the living mail order package.

and when erich with his dark eyes lights a cigarette, then it's as if it had always been in his face, as if it belonged exactly there, and not as a foreign body in a tired, furrowed face sticky with sweat and with dirty blond or mousey hair above it, as one sees so often now.

as long as paula had been a child, erich had only treated her like a child, now paula must make him realise, that she is no longer a child, but already a proper woman.

at some point we were already at the place, where erich comes into paula's parents' kitchen, the white cigarette in the brown face, above it the jet-black hair and eyes, an exotic figure like a panther, a little like a panther.

paula once read about certain men, who in ordinary surroundings seemed like panthers in a jungle.

exotic, dangerous and a pleasure to the eye and heart.

she had never believed that she herself would one day have a man in her ordinary kitchen who would seem like a dangerous panther in a dangerous jungle. but if someone could, then erich, the panther. immediately paula looks in the weekend magazine for the passage with the panther, there it is!

paula also learned english. she was the best at english and arithmetic. and good at other subjects too. but that's no use to her now.

erich didn't complete school, which doesn't matter. because he is like a beautiful wild animal: a panther.

paula knows, that erich is everything. so she herself must become much more, otherwise something else will get in far ahead of her. But how? but how?

paula, the little nothing, shoots around like a rocket, zigzag, makes coffee, fetches the guglhopf, actually intended for dada and gerald and therefore hidden. the full broadside of the two disappointed men will, it is true, strike paula before the day is out, but by then the cake will already by in erich's body. paula buzzes around like a bee. in his ponderous slow way erich tries to say that paula is already a proper little housewife.

paula once preferred good dressmaking to bad housework. now suddenly she is puffing herself up like a wood pigeon, coos around, ruffles her plumage, displays all her finery, lowers her eyelids, and hauls over everything in her reach, apart from the holy water font a lot can be put to use for erich.

erich is good at putting fodder to use. he eats until he's sick. erich is only interested in engines, that is, in ones that are fitted on a moped or, even better, on a motor cycle. erich would so terribly much like to get his driving licence, so that he can also be interested in more powerful engines, which are his secret love, that is, for sports cars etc. but he has already failed his driving test three times.

it is possible that since his earliest childhood his family has unanimously and systematically beaten the motor centre in his head to pieces, irreparable.

never again will erich be able to be unreservedly happy. erich's happiness will always remain limited. paula on the other hand will never be happy at all.

erich is not very interested in the cinema, in which paula is very interested, because everything happens too fast for him.

the female summer visitors too have departed so quickly again for unknown far away lands.

what is far away is dangerous, what is nearby is familiar, one can really grow fond of it. there is nothing near erich, that he could grow fond of. near erich there is only paula.

if erich could choose between paula and a motor cycle, he would take the motor cycle. even with a motor cycle erich only goes as far as the next village and no further, to more distant lands.

paula skims the milk, to make whipped cream.

the women in paula's family are famous for their cleanliness. otherwise there is nothing positive to be reported about the women in paula's family. that's why it's worth living, that's something one can always improve on: cleanliness. come on paula, on with the cleaning!

slow erich sits on the bench and eats enough for three.

everything, that at home only dada gets. he stuffs the cake down his throat as if it's his confirmation party, pours coffee after it and schnapps from the secret drawer. slow erich spreads like a plant over the bench and on the bench, eats and eats, and is thinking of nothing else except his engines, his moped, that can go so incredibly fast, above all when he's had a drink.

but he still doesn't understand how it all fits together yet, because the parts fit together so complicatedly.

despite that erich dreams of a much faster machine, of the feeling of movement, of speed, of a super engine, but if only one little thing on the fucking moped is broken, then right away he has to go to his friend, he's an expert, admittedly he works in the forest too, but a genius in the forest, he then fixes it for him for a couple of beers. a talent, going to waste in the forest.

erich would best of all like to take apart his moped and put it together again as a racing car.

erich eats cake, it's like on sunday for his dada, erich thinks about the moped, which he has, about his motor cycle, which he will have one day, so that he can then think about a car. and about the car, about which he thinks, so that one day, sometime one day in the future, he can think about a sports car, about which he can already read a great deal and pictures of which he can look at.

has love come to paula today despite that or exactly because of it? paula tells love to take a seat, it'll get coffee with milk right away. but love does not sit down obediently, it digs its claws into paula, how will it all end? paula asks herself but not erich, this fool for engines.

hopefully in the better life, hopes paula as so often before.

hopefully as quickly as possible as far away as possible, hopes erich, and certainly not on foot, hopes erich.

what nice intercourse that was again!

yes, that was nice intercourse again, thinks heinz. he wipes his mouth, combs his hair, cleans his eyebrows, inside his ears, his nose, washes his hands, drinks his breakfast coffee and leaves the house, to carry on his job. right away, as soon as he leaves the house, he enters the stress of working life, enters the mysterious world of wires, which brigitte does not understand at all.

meanwhile brigitte follows her destiny as woman, which is easier and simpler than a man's destiny.

she opens her locker, takes off skirt and jumper and slips on a cotton work coat, which is bright and neat and is there to improve the work atmosphere, to introduce a little colour into the dreary grey and black of the machines. cheerful splashes of colour: sunbeams. after brigitte has improved the work atmosphere and worsened her own condition at the same time, she slips into the healthy wooden health sandals, so that her feet stay healthy at work and don't get sick like some feet do. but not brigitte's, she makes sure of that.

if one knows about scientific things like health, then one can prevent a great deal, even illnesses.

all her colleagues wear these sandals too. they too are doing something for the health of their feet. the wooden sandal is popular in this circle.

and brigitte's work on the line has already begun, before she's even had time to take a proper look. work on the line leaves brigitte her femininity, because it is a women's factory with only female employees (women workers), so it is not difficult to maintain cleanliness. the only males are the more senior positions, who one doesn't see and who therefore cannot spoil the feminine cleanliness.

in completely male factories sometimes something nasty is left lying around on the floor, without anyone immediately doing something about it. in the brassière factory only pretty things are left lying on the floor, sometimes a piece of lace, a salmon pink ribbon, though that too is eliminated immediately.

actually nothing at all is ever left lying on the floor. and the tables in the canteen! here too the advantage of cleanliness everywhere: so clean, that one could eat off them! the women and girls vie with one another to be the first to discover a speck of dirt or dust or a stain, already the stain is gone, sometimes it's already gone, before it's even appeared.

sometimes a coffee stain even has to be removed

from the white formica surface, afterwards everyone feels relieved about that.

if by chance one of the managerial staff passes through, who however never pass through, then the young stain has long ago breathed its last.

and neither should a secretary, who passes through by chance, be allowed to see a stain, because she knows all about stains, but never seems to cause any herself.

secretaries often have a hobby. these include travel, dancing, country walks cinema or handicrafts.

the men whom the seamstresses know are, apart from work, unfortunately only interested in how they can recover from this work. they have no hobbies. often they have bad hobbies, in which they don't include the family.

what the sales manager, the company secretary, the advertising manager and the technical manager are interested in is not known.

what they work at, is not exactly known either. the gentlemen are not from here.

on the brassière line it's difficult to have any interests apart from the brassière line, because often one does not know what interests even exist. one only knows, that one or more persons have an interest in keeping the line going.

even if one knows, that something else apart from work and the male workers exists, it must first of all occur to one, that the something else, that exists, could also be there for oneself and not only for the others.

brigitte at any rate is one of the few who has recognised that there is something that goes far beyond work. brigitte has recognised by chance, that there is more than just work, much more, that is: HEINZ.

by chance therefore brigitte has recognised, that apart from the work, which she doesn't want, her workmates, whom she cannot stand, because really she isn't one of them any more, whom she cannot stand at all for the very reason that her workmates believe her to be one of them, which she stopped being long ago, thanks to heinz, who's something better, simply the best, in fact, by chance therefore brigitte has recognised that in life apart from work, work, changing for work, making coffee, work etc., there is also the one and only, who has thoroughly ruined and spoiled all that for her, by chance brigitte has recognised HEINZ. heinz and everything that follows from that.

if one is sitting in brigitte's completely hopeless situation on the line, one can only recognize something better – heinz – by chance.

if one is sitting in brigitte's hopeless situation on the line, one can only get something better – heinz – by a completely improbable chance as well.

will chance be kind to brigitte?

while brigitte stretches her toes in her healthy health sandals, to keep even these healthy and fresh for heinz, she looks down on her fellow seamstresses from a dizzy height, in spirit already separated from them by an insuperable distance: brigitte the businesswoman.

the others, who only see shops from the inside and only when they buy baby food for their brood or a salami sausage for their husbands.

brigitte who will own the shop through heinz, knows, that property can weigh heavily, but can also be a pleasure, at least brigitte will then know, whom she will be slaving for, that is, for herself and heinz and not for an unknown anonymous unfriendly mass like here.

something of your own is something of your own.

that's how far, insanely far, brigitte's thoughts can sometimes wander!

heinz thinks about everything possible, least of all however about brigitte.

heinz thinks about the same things as brigitte, that is, about his own shop.

heinz hopes, that what he does with brigitte will have no consequences. when heinz thinks about brigitte, then not about her herself, but about the possible consequences. heinz weighs up b. against her consequences.

brigitte hopes, that what she does with heinz will have consequences, MUST have consequences.

there must be a little child! a horrible, white, clinging grub of an infant. for heinz it will be simply and succinctly: our child! it will embody the permanent bond, which b. is looking for.

heinz tries to prevent any permanent bond by every means possible. for heinz a baby would be a millstone around his neck, a hindrance, a drag on his promising development towards: businessman.

brigitte wants to get it inside her and, then that it also stays inside and doesn't dribble out again unused, pointless and without a future. brigitte wants heinz to discharge and shoot the extract of the roast beef and the bread dumplings from today's dinner into her. by now this slimy muck must at last have been squirted into her and be safe inside, but no, it takes time to do a thing well and heinz needs time too.

yes, it takes less than a second, who would have believed it, and a new little person is made.

take your time and don't kill yourself, or: take it easy, if you stay calm, you show your strength, heinz replies good-humouredly to brigitte's urgings. heinz remains calmly on top of brigitte with all his body weight pressing down on her and takes a break for a bit. his load is heavy and he does not make it any lighter.

brigitte feels heinz's bloated stomach pressing down on her, there is nothing to suggest that there is still life in this colossus.

heinz is not exactly the lightest, but he doesn't consider that. shall i kick him in the flanks like a horse, flashes briefly through brigitte.

heinz of course would like to prolong the few good moments, which one can have with brigitte, as long as possible. things just don't happen that fast and certainly not with heinz.

heinz is always ready with a pat reply.

as life and movement slowly return to heinz again, brigitte thinks about her future. the future is a distraction from the repellent present. brigitte wants heinz to do it faster, because perhaps the future can't wait much longer. the foreplay should be over and done with, so that the main part, the son and heir can begin.

heinz grunts and wallows.

what he's doing is not intended as foreplay for brigitte, rather heinz first has to get the hang of things, before he enters the final round.

any foreplay that brigitte would enjoy has never occurred to heinz.

only now does heinz get started, his engine is warm at last.

now heinz, who is a man of the moment, wants to have some fun.

heinz thrusts away like mad, so that the guts in his abdomen begin to spin.

that's just his character.

brigitte would like her enjoyment later, but an enjoyment that's all the more permanent instead.

love passes, but LIFE goes on.

only love lets us live!

paula, as one can gather from these rash words, sees a possibility of survival not only in the betterment of dressmaking, paula now also sees in love a possibility of LIVING. it seems to her, as if she must run a race over a long distance with the others, on a stretch which is full of holes in the ground, and all together they fall into the holes and are gone, like at billiards: her sister with her children and her ruined fingers, her brother, who will soon have children too and already has ruined fingers, erich's momma, who has a lot of children, it's a miracle she has any fingers left, all of them fall into the holes and disappear from the screen on which reality happens.

but she, paula, dodges the holes brilliantly! at the end of the distance comes the fall into erich's arms and the ringing of church bells.

end of dressmaking, beginning of the most real life, there is none more real. one does not need to think about dying for a long time, because death won't come for a long time, if life is real and proper. only if one lives an unreal and improper life like momma or dada, who are only born, begin to slave and then just die, without having felt the reality of real life, only if one leads this improper and unreal life, this life of work, from which one gets nothing, then one dies a real and lasting death. it happens so fast sometimes, that in the end one believes it was nothing at all.

suddenly paula sees dressmaking as her natural enemy. luckily she hasn't yet got involved with it so seriously and inextricably, that it would stick to her. luckily dressmaking is something one can jettison at any time. luckily dressmaking doesn't cling or hang on to one without letting go, as unreasonable people sometimes do, as paula would now like to do with erich. luckily dressmaking is not EVERYTHING, but love and a little house of one's own, that one must build.

paula wants erich, whom she'll get, whose child she'll get, whereupon she'll give away her job, so as to get more of erich's children, i.e. one more child.

paula won't get something for nothing.

before paula gets something for nothing, she'll lose everything.

paula will get a car then too, in return for which erich will get her herself, which isn't much, but which erich must not know, who must believe, that it's the most that he can get.

naturally one has to change him a little, before happiness can come at last and make its entry: erich must give up his drinking completely, because that's the worst, because it affects and concerns the white varnished kitchen furniture and the new walnut bedroom suite personally. alcohol and new furniture are natural enemies by nature. also alcohol and neat skirts, which must not be puked over, white shoes which look like genuine leather, but are not, and nevertheless must not be puked over, children in bright coloured little dresses, pot plants, the television with the plastic flowers in the plastic vase, all that and alcohol, curtains of transparent synthetic fibre and alcohol, non-iron textiles and alcohol, these are simply enemies in nature, wherever they meet. enemies.

all white and soft things go together in paula's head, alcohol does not go with them. alcohol disturbs and destroys.

now one mustn't forget the present when thinking about the future. but naturally one must not (serious mistake!) completely lose sight of the future when thinking about the present.

paula's present is no longer dressmaking, paula's present is her love of erich, which will also suffice for the whole of her future.

since love is therefore real life, paula's unreal life must be changed in such a way that it becomes real and full of love. this is how it's done:

you have often seen in the cinema, erich, haven't you, that between extraordinary people extraordinary things like for example an extraordinary love can arise. so we only have to be extraordinary and see what happens. the people all around are ordinary, they do nothing but work and work. we who do nothing but work, but also love one another, are extraordinary. we no longer need to look for the extraordinary, because we already have it: our love.

sometimes it only happens once in a lifetime, if one doesn't take it with both hands, then one will be very unhappy, if e.g. one lets the beloved woman or the beloved man go far away or astray. love is different from what one experiences or has otherwise, at work or at home.

because otherwise we don't have anything.

but love, we have that. so hold on tight to happiness! at this moment as at so many others before erich is thinking about the distributor head and the carburettor, which he can't tell apart anyway, after that erich thinks without a break, although it's an effort, about the exterior of the whole thing: about the bodywork, about steering and driving.

paula thinks for two however and right away thinks further ahead, almost in instalments. no longer about love and what happens in the body and/or changes in it, but about the new apartment, the children and the snack with coffee and cream for the OTHERS, whom one has to SHOW something.

sometimes (rarely) erich also thinks about the complicatedly written magazines about the last world war. one often does not know anything at all about many of the events in them any more. the breath of history touches erich. erich rarely thinks about women.

erich never thinks about paula, unless he has to, because she happens to be there.

paula thinks about her cuddly soft son. paula thinks about a white hospital room. paula thinks about her old family, which in paula's new life at most fits into a hospital room, as visitors and in their very best sunday clothes. the very best thing that paula can think of, is how her family will regret the thrashings, which they gave her in a worse life.

when the photographs have been taken, the family

will leave the hospital room again as one man. after that erich will present red roses, which will not be dreams and shadows, but a dream that came true.

of course envy will also be there to give congratulations.

as we can see there exists a great difference between paula's present and paula's future, as well as between erich's present and erich's future, as well as between paula's present and erich's present, as well as between paula's future and erich's future, an even larger one exists however between paula's present and erich's future, and between erich's present and paula's future.

how can these phenomena of world importance be made to match up?

then begins the work, which one person must perform and which the other person then appropriates. then begins the work, which the other person must perform, and which the first person then appropriates. that both work simultaneously and then equally profit by it is out of the question in this case. too dissimilar are the standpoints, too unequally distributed the advantages and disadvantages, too great is erich's advantage because of his physical assets and his gender. that is due to erich's physical strength and appearance, which is admired above all by women, who are the ones to be chosen.

erich is something like paula's father or paula's brother or paula's brother-in-law, something that hands out beatings and gets drunk, even if until now he had hardly any opportunity to do so, because until now he himself has only been beaten; but if he now soon gets an opportunity, with a woman that is, which he does not know yet.

beating people is fun, which erich does not know yet.

paula on the other hand. paula on the other hand has to bear all the disadvantages of her appearance and her gender. paula is not regarded as pretty, as which a woman must be regarded, but she is regarded as pure.

cleanliness and purity can enhance the value of a female person, but don't necessarily.

whereas dressmaking is superfluous, does not belong here, did not have to put in an appearance at all, will anyway soon vanish from the scene, will no longer count, whereas this dressmaking is completely inessential, compared to life and the love in it, whereas this dressmaking is completely pointless, cannot replace a man and not prepare a woman for a man, is no use to a woman, if she already has a man and doesn't get her a man if she needs one, whereas this dressmaking doesn't make one HAPPY, which only a man can do.

paula is not worth more because she is training as a dressmaker. but because she is always clean, that can make her worth more, almost pretty, which one has to be, in order to experience love.

paula would have had fun doing dressmaking, but reality after all is serious.

erich's manliness, good looks and his wage as a woodcutter against paula's femininity, ugliness, but cleanliness. and against paula's apprenticeship allowance. erich's love of fast engines of every kind against paula's love of erich. erich's love of the adventures of the second world war against paula's love of erich. erich's love of fast motor cycles and sports cars against paula's love of erich and a house of their

own. erich's preference for fast things against paula's preference for love and for erich. they are the same thing to paula.
life and erich.

when they are out walking brigitte

lovingly-possessively takes hold of heinz's hand. at every moment, which does not happen to belong to work, brigitte attempts lovingly-possessively to take hold of heinz's hand, sometimes she has to walk alongside him for hours before she even gets a chance to offer her hand. but then firmly, straight, so that she doesn't plant a kiss on it.
taking his hand is important above all when other women are present and turn up as danger made flesh and bone. shyly then a little hand slips into heinz's big one and talks about the weather, the world situation or about food or about nature. sometimes heinz plainly acts as if he and brigitte were not one person, which they are however. do these women not see that in reality we are one, have become one, inseparable, asks brigitte in astonishment when other women look at heinz as a separate body with a separate spirit.
when other women regard heinz as something, that one could still get, when he's no longer to be had, because brigitte already has him, then these other women are in the wrong and on the wrong track. to each his own.
leisure time without heinz would not be leisure. work without heinz is full of dangers for heinz and for brigitte. work without heinz is nothing but an obstacle on brigitte's way to heinz.

it is unbelievable, how much one can hate someone. brigitte only needs to look at heinz and already she hates him again.

brigitte also hates heinz among other things, because he always lets a physical feeling for brigitte rise, just when gitti would like to talk about her emotional problems, which involve a little house with a garden. whenever brigitte wants to turn her innermost to the outside and spew out all the crap about happiness, future, baby care and washing machines, then heinz acts as if he didn't have a brain, but only a cock.

surely heinz doesn't just see a body when he looks at brigitte and not all the variety behind it?

brigitte has even already referred to wars and internal crises to explain, that one human being must have another, who in turn helps the other to get over these.

my god, how i hate you for that, thinks b.

heinz is happy at last to have found a person to rut. hardly has heinz set eyes on the person brigitte, than he's unbuttoning himself and going into the starting position. while brigitte is still explaining to him, that she loves him and at the same time feels something like respect for his professional success, while brigitte is still letting her thoughts wander from love and respect to wedding and house renovation, before she even has time to watch out, she already has heinz the rutter clinging to her body like a leech.

and heinz operates his pump handle diligently.

brigitte's mother gives the good advice that brigitte must not let go again. as brigitte's stomach turns and turns, heinz does not let go again, holds on tight, breathes rotten bad teeth breath up gitti's sensitive

nose and sprays drops of spittle generously over eyelids screwed up in disgust.

yes, heinz has come, with all the desires and demands
that such a heinz brings with him.

mummy has gone to the cinema, and in steps heinz,
and unleashes his cock on brigitte.

brigitte wishes it would curl up, that would certainly
cause heinz a lot of sorrow. meanwhile brigitte has a
lot of sorrow.

it does not occur to brigitte to say leave me in
peace.

brigitte knows, there are so many woman who would
like to turn a stranger's, her, brigitte's future into
one of their own.

so brigitte prefers to turn herself into an extension
of heinz's limbs, into a part of heinz's body.

hardly has heinz shot through the door, than he's
already aiming at the settee, even before he's taken
off his pullover, he's already taking a blind leap, brigitte cushions the onslaught with her body.

perhaps one day heinz will have so much momentum
that he simply tears through brigitte and through the
wall on the other side. today heinz has only just
enough momentum, so that he skilfully positions it
in brigitte. it is a masterpiece of precision. it is torture
for brigitte.

brigitte doesn't even dare to say, if she's hungry or
thirsty. if heinz is hungry later, then brigitte is too, a
single body in every respect. heinz and brigitte are
one.

a happy situation for two young people.

brigitte hates heinz fervently.

in one of the numerous passionate situations which
heinz brings about, without considering how revolt-

ing this might be for brigitte, brigitte could for example instead of holding out her snatch hold out a sack, which is full of long thorns, and heinz hops in, heave ho, works his way in with tail up, there's no stopping him! straight into the thorns or nails! that would certainly be no fun, how helplessly his legs would wriggle in the air!

brigitte has to smile at the idea.

heinz does not know why b. thinks it's funny when he sinks down on her like an eclipse or other natural catastrophe.

b. lets heinz go on believing in the natural force of nature.

b. groans dreadfully and heartbreakingly. cause: his natural force.

brigitte feels nothing but a strangely unpleasant scraping inside her. brigitte feels love inside her.

heinz groans too, so that brigitte sees, what an effort he is making for her and how strong he is.

heinz groans with strength, but not with love.

heinz won't stand for much nonsense when it comes to love, and when it comes to strength he'll stand for none at all.

because if one wants to open a shop of one's own, one has to rely completely on oneself, at most perhaps someone else contributes (start-up) money at the beginning.

brigitte won't stand for any nonsense when it comes to love. it is the most serious thing which she, entirely without start-up money, can do for her own shop.

brigitte and heinz groan in a two part harmony of love.

brigitte has an unpleasant feeling in her body, heinz a pleasant one.

for brigitte her body counts as a means to a better end.

for heinz his body counts a lot, more than anything, that is, apart from his professional advancement. and good food!

it's fun for heinz, but not for brigitte.

heinz has fun, although he won't stand for any nonsense.

brigitte gets nothing out of it apart from a vague hope. apart from that brigitte has a vagina. which she makes use of. brigitte's vagina snaps greedily at the young entrepreneur.

a physical union is in progress between brigitte and heinz. brigitte says, it's so good with you, that one would like to die. heinz is very proud of this sentence, he repeats it again and again to his friends.

it's so good with you, heinz, that one would like to die. at any rate i would not like to die at work, heinz, if it has to be, then let it be before that at least.

paula's preferences

paula's preference for life and for erich. they are the same thing for paula. so let's get on with both of them!

however when erich at last leaves the clean kitchen of paula's parents, engines in his heart, guglhopf cake and schnapps in his stomach, not a thing in his head, because he has said everything he was supposed to say, he has no memory at all of a living person, of paula, only a hazy memory of a woman, who did to him, what women have always done to him, that is, gave him something to eat, gave him something to eat, gave him something to eat, waited on him back and front like a statue of a saint, one sets down flower pots for. hence no memory of any person at all, only a memory of the results of this person, that is pleasant warmth in the stomach from schnapps and a sweet feeling of being full, likewise in the stomach, of cake. and the coffee wasn't bad either, not instant.

all of that is for erich quite separate from what he always does with the female summer visitors, who for him are already much more real living persons, because they are constantly able to decide between many different possibilities, e.g. whether one drives to the waterfall or up into the mountains, or whether one goes dancing or to play skittles. so much free decision-making scares erich.

but these summer visitors are a quite different kind of woman or they are women, and momma and paula are perhaps not women or the other way round, so they are a quite different kind of woman, who don't constantly stick something in front of one, who don't look after one, but who themselves want something stuck into them, but who nevertheless often have money, but are not women to be married, as many from hearsay say.

in contrast to: women for marrying who only want to have something stuck in when they've been married, but which nevertheless very few of them can persevere with long enough, till success is achieved. so: erich therefore thinks of two kinds of women, when he thinks about women at all, which he only does, when he feels a need, which one cannot satisfy by thinking anyway. erich therefore thinks about women, who are not women to him, because like his sexless momma they constantly shove food and drink into him, and about women, who are not women to him, because to him they are not allowed to be women, because they do it with anybody, without being in love, engaged or married to him and would be quite incapable of keeping a whole house clean.

although very few women have a whole house. although it's all the same to erich whether there's a woman or not or none.

erich doesn't think about women anyway, or if he does, then only about women who aren't women at all, that's why for erich there are no women, because the women he knows are in reality not women at all. erich feels the results of women, but not the women themselves. that's why and for many other reasons as well erich thinks exclusively about his machines.

that's why and for many other reasons as well paula is at this moment thinking about erich and how she can become his wife, which will be difficult, but yet must be possible.

subsequently dressmaking, which was something better, and has now suddenly, without being able to understand why, become something dull and not so good, groans loudly in pain: paula, if you don't pay more attention to me than you are paying attention to me now, then i can no longer be the better life for you as originally was my intention. then suddenly, without you even properly noticing, i will not be able to be a little piece of your life any more.

but paula doesn't listen properly to dressmaking, which is something better, any more.

because while paula is carrying out the dressmaking, she is thinking about the best life, which will certainly be there much more quickly with erich than the better life with dressmaking, which will only be there

in two years, when she has finished her apprenticeship. but the best life can perhaps already begin
tomorrow!

paula, be prepared at all times.

the best is still better than the better.

better, that one sees one's happiness in another
person than oneself, as momma, grandmomma, her
sister have already looked for happiness in someone
else and by no means found it, better one sees one's
happiness in someone else and finds it there too
than that one makes one's happiness oneself or one
doesn't find one's happiness, and the days of one's
youth are over.

better, happiness is made from a human being than
from inhuman silk, cotton or inhuman linen.

how does one become a woman for erich, whom he
can also recognise as woman? no more seams, no
button holes, no *à jour* stitches, no herringbone stitches, no cross stitches, or only half heartedly.

erich mows grass for fodder.

erich mows grass for fodder.

today is already the hundred thousandth day on
which erich mows grass for fodder. as well as the
work in the forest erich always has to mow grass for
fodder. and carry out many other jobs, like mow
grass for fodder, muck out, spread muck on the
meadow, mow grass for fodder, once again, mow
grass for fodder one last time and much more
besides.

paula visits erich's momma and the persons around
her, who are really people around erich, everything
revolves around erich, the centre of attention, who
mows grass for fodder, as if he did that every day.

good afternoon, i've brought a cake with regards from my momma. i hope you enjoy it.

erich's momma is surprised, because it is not usual, if one has something, that one voluntarily gives away even one little piece of it, that has never happened before, because here everyone tries to get, but doesn't want to give anything in return, because here every-one tries as hard as possible to get something for nothing. but because in general one knows that one simply CANNOT get something for nothing, not even serious illnesses, so erich's momma is surprised when suddenly a cake simply walks into the house for nothing. thank you very much. kind regards. but since as has been said, the chance of getting some-thing for nothing, is one in a million, then erich's momma immediately thinks a bit more. what is it that this girl can want in return? what is there of value that we own, which she can imagine even for a second, that we would give it away, that she could get it? it must be something, that is at least a touch more valuable than the cake, after all one always wants to get back more than one has invested. she can't seriously imagine that we would give away any-thing, even if it were the dirt under our nails, for nothing, because for a piece of cake she gets at most a piece of fatty smoked meat, the lean we eat our-selves, and she has never claimed that she would like to have a piece of smoked meat or a couple of eggs or a jar of stewed plums. surely she doesn't want some of the home-made jam? for that she'll have to bring cakes up till she's black in the face, when i think how much work that jam was. she can eat her own jam!

paula is taking her life in her hands. until now she's

only reaping misunderstanding, ingratitude and mistrust for it.

nevertheless paula is very active. she picks the flowers for as long as they are blooming and perhaps even before. because then they open up in the tumbler or in the pretty porcelain vase in one's own little room. and only oneself has the benefit of it or a welcome visitor.

but there comes the day, on which it becomes clear that it cannot be the jam. because if it had been the jam, then paula would already have said something about jam after the eighth piece of cake. she can't be as daft as to carry up ten pieces of cake for a jar of jam, when she could get a jar of jam for eight pieces of cake!

so what does paula want, what is it that she wants so much of?

erich is yet again mowing grass for fodder. can i help you to carry the fodder, asks paula. she isn't dressed for carrying fodder, more for church, which she never goes to however, because her parents never go either, because one doesn't get anything for it. erich looks at paula as one looks at a harmless beetle, which one doesn't absolutely have to crush underfoot, if one's in a good mood. erich doesn't look at paula angrily. erich looks at paula and again doesn't look at her. you'll get grass marks on your dress, he says, because you look as if you wanted to go to church. you could go off to church right now, the way you look. no, i'll help you, erich, you always have to work so hard! yes, the work is certainly hard, but it's good to do it in the fresh open air, i would die in these factories in that stale shut in air, in which even women are said to work, who are after all fairly weak, erich puts in.

you are right, paula replies to what erich has said, there is a changed atmosphere between them, an atmosphere of harmony. work in the open air is supposed to be healthier than work in the factory, i've read that too.

erich hasn't read it, because he only reads magazines about the war, but erich too has heard that work in the fresh air is healthier and less restricted. you're right, paula throws in, the fresh air and working in it give one strength, health and rosy cheeks. but you are strong, erich. and healthy. this was the first real conversation between erich and paula, a conversation in which one person says something and the other replies, with something whose meaning fits. at this moment the thought shoots through erich, paula could be a person just as he is.

erich has fleetingly grasped the crux of the problem. where his mother is concerned, erich overlooks the crux of the problem. erich only feels the effect of his mother: making food, cleaning up, cursing, threatening a beating, cleaning up and once more making food.

paula has given an answer to something erich has said.

erich has directly experienced the consequences of one of his actions.

in return paula can help carry the basket.

that is the moment, at which erich and paula do something together for the first time, that is carry a basket with grass for fodder.

if erich and paula do something in future, then they will lock themselves in to do it or go into the woods.

no one must be allowed to observe them in future, when they do something together.

sometimes paula and erich also complement one another in future, for example when erich batters and paula is battered, or when erich is sick and paula nurses him or when they both saw wood together, or when paula cooks and erich eats.

often popular opinion tells merry jokes about people like paula. ultimately these jokes say that however dumb women may be, they're still darlings none the less.

but they're still darlings none the less.

in other places the jokes also say, that, however brutal, sly, cunning and crafty men may be, they're still darlings none the less.

but they're still darlings none the less.

at this moment erich's mother begins to think about the basket carrying. this time it happens quickly, although erich's mother has an unpractised brain.

paula wants neither butter nor cheese, nor milk nor wine nor jam. paula wants that person who is substantially involved in the production of these products, with his money and his labour power: that is erich.

but they're still darlings none the less.

NO! thinks erich's momma.

one day brigitte and heinz were

at it again, and heinz unzipped the zip fastener on her back, suddenly all of brigitte's back was revealed in the daylight. it's not that beautiful that it can be exposed to bright light, says heinz.

nevertheless, moved by so much unnecessary enthusiasm, he takes brigitte in his car out to his parents' little summer house.

if one has a little summer house, that's already something, but it's possible to go higher to a detached or semi-detached house. the summer house, as small as it is, is supposed to be an incentive to heinz, that it's possible to go even higher. don't propose and let god dispose, rather let others propose, but dispose oneself.

daddy and mummy know what's good for heinz.

that's why they're pleased to see susi the grammar school girl enter their common life.

susi therefore enters fully into their life and thereby simultaneously threatens the life that is not yet emergent, but should be emergent in brigitte.

susi is refined, not brigitte.

one cannot compare the two of them. that's impossible.

one can like one or the other, heinz must make the decision.

does he prefer this or that.

if he decides for susi and refinement, his parents will give him some nice initial capital for the marriage, that is their entire savings from their entire life together. it's not much, but it's nice.

brigitte goes to the factory to her piece rate target. susi goes to the girls' grammar school to her cookery classes. susi is already a proper little woman with all the little faults and weaknesses, which a woman has, and which her own mother has taught her with a painstaking attention to detail, that is many weaknesses. hardly has one bumped into susi, than she's already talking about recipes. she moves in a world in which conversations about recipes are the order of the day. today for example she is saying, that while the last almond biscuits looked attractive, they tasted awful. despite that her daddy ate some, so as not to hurt his little daughter, because after all her cooking is her pride and joy. she had made such an effort and even spread egg white on them, so that they shine nicely, and now they look nice, but taste bad, yuck. her big brother hans complains too in his grammar school way, in which the word shit often occurs, which brigitte also feels burning in her mouth all this time. let it out brigitte, let the shit out, otherwise you'll choke on it!

daddy said: keep on practising your cooking, susanne, yesterday, the noodles, they may have looked horrible, but to make up for it they were so tasty, well, they were as tasty as if they'd been made by a real little housewife. and then my daddy said, chatters susi to heinz, who is lying in the deck chair, then daddy said, since you are already a proper little woman, susi, one has to deal leniently with these almond biscuits, but since you are still a little girl, that is daddy's little girl, you must be punished. no going out tonight. and we'll practise cooking together, then you'll be another step closer to a housewife.

the end.

heinz's parents don't stop beaming, at last a gleam on the horizon. susi's family is absolutely pregnant with future, with one son at boys' grammar school and one even at university! hopefully our heinz is equipped for that. still, we've given him good tools.

a solid apprenticeship and thoughts of a business of his own.

the two of them got to know each other at the open air swimming pool, a point of contact of many interests, a point of intersection of all classes, opinions and trends.

susi is a person who has interests. susi is interested in paperbacks and cinema. susi is interested in people who are interested in the same or similar paperbacks and films. so then one can choose and decide between various paperbacks and films. susi is interested in whatever is the same, for what she already is. it is virtually the job of a lifetime to decide between two different films, both of which one would like to see. one immediately has the feeling, that the universe revolves around one.

susi is also very interested in cooking. there is nothing to be said about that, because it's right and proper. for the whole of mankind, which susi sometimes also touches on in conversation.

susi can touch on things, because she has a broad view of things. if one asks susi light or dark, then she replies: middle.

and laughs sweetly.

susi is something middling, which is safest, because it's not up and not down. in the middle one neither has to take too much pressure nor perform too much groundbreaking work.

in the girls' grammar school, that's the right place to be.

beside the right man, that's the right place to be. the right man is like or a little or if possible much better than oneself. with a man one's in the wrong place, if

he is below one's own level. susi's level is high, so
susi thinks.

susi immediately in no time at all sized up everything
in sight. susi learned that from her mother, who all
day long does nothing but assess, measure, weigh up
and count. result: lower. a hard but final word.

nevertheless it's interesting for a girl like susanne,
who's eager to learn, to look down on so many different people, who are fundamentally almost identical
with one another, are the same, that is on a level far
below susi, in a single heap.

while susi measures and weighs up, she stretches
femininely in the deck chair. susi is not a little girl
any more, but already a proper woman, which one
clearly notices when she stretches.

susi feels tolerant of brigitte. out of tolerance susi
would like to initiate brigitte into her cooking skills,
for which she earns only ingratitude and misunderstanding. a little put out susi is silent again. a shame
on such a beautiful clear day.

brigitte immediately feels sick, if she even catches
sight of susi's lily-white beach robe and her long
blonde hair. that is an interesting reaction, which is
completely different from heinz's reaction. heinz has
recognised susi's quality. after all he's going to be a
good businessman one day. brigitte cannot recognise
quality, that's why one day she may go under.

susi doesn't feel brigitte's hate at all, because her
thoughts revolve around jam tarts and larded saddle
of venison. all hatred is foreign to susi. susi is friendly
and home-loving.

all the assembled summer house owners and gar-
deners think that susi is a little bit interested in them,

because she is so friendly. but that's not so. susi is not interested in them.

it's simply, that heinz and his parents are often coarse and impolite, which they should think about, because there is no need to be unfriendly. so thinks sunny susi.

in brigitte's circles one hates any competition. in brigitte's circles hate is writ large. brigitte cannot summon up any love for her fellow women, it has all been destroyed.

in susi's circle love rules, which should rule the whole world, and before which hate should fall silent. susi is very nice to b., because she is no more interested in brigitte than in a piece of rotting wood. brigitte hates susi as one can only hate something that wears a lily-white beach robe.

brigitte has to show susi the garden and the fruit trees. susi claps her hands with pleasure. brigitte trembles before each plum tree, for god's sake, she surely doesn't want to take this from me, which almost already belongs to me, that is, this tree, this, this and this away from me! i'll kill you, if you take away my future fruit trees, which are already almost mine, if you take away my future life, which is called heinz, if you take away my future house, which is called brigitte-and-heinz, if you take all that away from me, then i'll kill you, you can be sure of that.

susi walks happily through the grass with a spring in her step. carelessly she treads down michaelmas daisies, dahlias and lesser garden flowers, snap. brigitte throws herself on the ground and carefully straightens michaelmas daisies, dahlias and lesser garden flowers again, hopefully nothing is irreparably bent. hopefully, susi will be kicked out now that she's done that.

brigitte protects her property, that one day will be hers, with her whole body. if one has never had one's own property, then one fights for a presumptive property as if for one's own life. she throws herself across the currant bushes, to protect them from susi's hand, which impudently was about to pick a berry. in doing so b. crushes several pounds of the red berries with her clumsy body. that will cost her her head!

susi is astonished. she says, i can buy the berries anywhere, if i want to. brigitte says, yes, but these berries here, these are mine. MINE. mine. what's mine is mine.

and heinz is mine. mine. mine.

and one day i shall have a house, that is much more beautiful than this simple summer house, which we will leave to my parents-in-law, while we, heinz, who is mine, and i, who am also mine, will move into a bigger, more beautiful house, the ground floor of which will accommodate our own shop. an electrician's. thus far brigitte.

you've got yourself completely dirty, says susi in a friendly way, she is quite indifferent to brigitte. as far as susi is concerned it doesn't matter if b. exists or not. brigitte's existence does not affect susi's life in any way. susi is very nice to brigitte, because it doesn't cost anything, and brigitte can't take anything from her, not even her cooking skills.

brigitte however hates everything about susi. susi's existence is a constant threat. if heinz is once shown something better, he may possibly then also want to own it. NO!

susi wants to TAKE something from her.

what b. would most like to do is throw herself in front of heinz, the garden, the house as she did in front of the currant bushes, protect them from susi's impudent fingers with her own body.

susi points at the beauty of a sunflower. how pretty, says susi. pretty as a cake.

b. is deaf to the beauties of landscape. b. is not capable of taking in beauty, b. is completely twisted, knotted, like a rope. b. is a solid pile of hate. for b. there is nothing beautiful, only something, that one wants to get and must get.

in free verse susi lists various beauties of the plant world and some that taste good.

susi has a well-developed sense of beauty, her daddy says that too. brigitte only wants to have something. susi only wants to lose nothing. b. wants to own, own, own, otherwise everything is over and finished. b. fights. susi is too feminine to fight. susi is all woman.

susi gets.

brigitte is nothing at all.

continued: paula's feelings

so there is something inside me, which is called love, paula feels for the tenth time.

there is furthermore something inside me, that wishes to have children. one must not fight it.

at earliest at that moment, in which i shall become a mother, dressmaking will lose its last chance. with dressmaking, everything is quite dead, with a little child, everything is very much alive. it is love personified. what is dead dressmaking against a living child.

hopefully it won't be a stillbirth!

living things come first, then lifeless tools.

and so that one is not alone in old age.

erich thinks about things with engines, which are also very much alive. a racing car for example has the strength of several tigers.

it is an elegant unity of form and movement.

in his clearest moments erich thinks about a life with clean hands, white shirts, tight jeans and light work. or no work.

erich doesn't for a single second think about paula. he takes paula just as much for granted as the air he breathes. paula does not want to be taken for granted, but to be something special.

that's why paula crosses the street in a pinafore dress she has sewn herself. paula grinds her teeth with cleanliness. her hair, her dress, her shopping bag, her thin legs, all shine as if competing with one another in cleanliness, like a white whirlwind.

but that's just about all that's special about paula.

lifeless women like squashed may-flies sit on every threshold, sit there as if stuck on with liquid asphalt and ceaselessly survey their own little housewife kingdoms, in which they are queens. sometimes a washing-up liquid makes them queen, sometimes a shiny pressure cooker.

the front gardens are neatly fenced in and separated from the outside world. sunflowers and shrubbery separate the inner world from the outer world, which is hostile.

sometimes several families live together in small houses. paula too will get one of these, in whose kitchen paula can then reign, where everything will flash and sparkle, so that it makes everyone who sees it glad.

paula walks past and thinks up degrees of cleanliness. now and then one of the lifeless women jumps in front of paula and pulls one of her offspring, a son or a daughter to her bosom, as a bulwark, a figurehead against clean and single paula. over there one throws herself over her son, whom paula asked how he was getting on at school. she interrupts the son and proudly talks about all the problems she has with him, she is proud of the problems with her wild son, she is ashamed of the problems she has with her daughter. she says, that someone who has no children, can have no idea, what it's like, if one has some.

she also explains, that she is happy no longer to have to be a sales assistant, because it is unsatisfactory, to work for strangers. she was led to the altar straight from the shop counter.

now she has several dangerous looking symptoms of illness.

the doctor can find nothing.

she has found happiness.

she is happy that everything she does for her husband, is at the same time done for herself. the fresh socks, clean shirts, underpants and shoes, she does all of that for herself too and for the children. it is not possible for her to do something for herself in the first instance.

sometimes she goes to the hairdresser. it looks prettier.

when paula asks one of the women, what she would like, then she would like something for the whole family, for example, a car, in which then the whole family sits, and in which the mother is forever waiting to get a chance to smack the child's fingers, to be able to justify her own presence.

apart from that one can also decorate a car with little flower vases and cushions. it looks prettier.

somewhere in some house a child whose knuckles have been rapped is always bellowing. if one stops, another one starts up right away.

smacking sounds emerge from the gleaming windows.

paula says: don't hit karli so hard, he hasn't done anything, leave him alone.

paula should keep her mouth shut, because she hasn't given birth to anything at all yet.

the grandmomma's role is the soothing role.

that's why granny is liked so much by the children. granny is always disliked by husband and wife, because she interferes.

her own husband, the grandad, hates granny, first of all because he always already hated her when he was younger, which is an old much-loved habit, which one cannot give up so easily, and one keeps up this hatred in old age, because what does one have in old age after all, nothing except one's good old tried and tested hate.

and the hate grows ever bigger, because the granny has long ago lost her only capital, a beauty which was perhaps present. granny was devalued. grandad, the worn out old duffer, long ago lost the other younger women to other worn out but younger men, who are still able to earn a living.

the younger women won't risk their secure existence

at the side of these younger men for an old bugger like him.

so grandad too dies away, more slowly and more drawn-out than his almost-dead wife, but anyhow: dying is dying, lost is lost and gone. and one's own wife will always remind one of the decline from young lad to dirty old man.

grandad is used up, granny is being worn out. there is no user in sight, and yet one is being used up.

but granny knows very well that from a certain age the husband will be left to her for ever and ever, until the final fatal illness and the subsequent decease. he can no longer escape from her, from the cooker, from the sideboard, from the table, from the sink, from the feeding trough.

where else can the old crook go?

the old crook is dependent on her shitty grub.

and so a long string of shitty pants and sweaty socks continues to pass through granny's hands.

in her old age granny takes her revenge with little things. she has many opportunities for constructive revenge.

and so a string of hurts, which one can cause granny, continue to pass through grandad's hands, a string of dreadful days. grandad takes every single day, which granny still has to suffer, in his own hands. in person. no one else is allowed to interfere.

but since childhood grandad has been used to having his granny provide all the basic necessities, or his momma or his granny. he cannot even boil an egg himself.

he is dependent as a child, when it comes to the pleasant little things like household chores, one can easily turn him livid with rage with little things, with tiny discomforts, with acts of sabotage.

the old married couple are locked together like two insects, like two animals, who are eating one another up, one already half inside the body of the other.

flesh is nutritious and very patient.

in the distance a band of younger women pass by like a camel caravan, their silhouettes standing out sharply against the horizon. they are bearing full shopping bags and drag small children behind them.

dadda observes them lustfully through his binoculars.

a few remnants of manliness stir in his trousers.

momma screeches in the kitchen, and the remnants must fall silent again.

the sun is going down at last.

but paula, the stupid cow, has to love somebody!

as if it were not hard enough, even without it, to have a little detached house with its own garden. but *with* a little house it's much easier after all, thinks paula.

paula's body will do its utmost.

the sun has gone down at last.

despite that, the night too will bring yet more terrible things for man and wife.

but paula, the stupid cow, has to love somebody.

brigitte hates heinz

although brigitte hates heinz, she still wants to get him, so that he belongs to her completely and to no one else.

if b. already hates heinz now, before she has even got

him, how much more will she hate him, once, which is still very doubtful, she will have got him for ever and ever, and no longer has to make an effort to get him.

in the meantime however brigitte must carefully conceal her hate, because she is still nobody, that is a seamstress of brassières, and would like to become somebody, that is heinz's wife.

many other seamstresses come from yugoslavia, hungary, czechoslovakia or other countries of the eastern bloc.

or they get married and leave or they go to rack and ruin.

one out of very many is basically no one at all.

b. thinks, that, as one of very many brassière seamstresses, of whom many even sew the same seam as her, she is nobody at all. b. thinks that, as one of very many wives, she would be somebody. brigitte thinks, because heinz is somebody, that is somebody, who one day will be somebody, who has his own business, that she then automatically will be somebody too.

if no glitter comes from the brassières, then all the glitter in life must come from heinz.

because the glitter, which one reads about or which one sees on tv, comes from some quite different person and returns to some quite other person, because the glitter from the magazines and films deals with people who are complete strangers, who often don't even wear brassières, never mind make brassières, so because there is no glitter from the start, b. industriously makes glitter. for hours on end. and always around heinz. she hopes, that something of this glitter will be reflected back at her. but whoever has glitter, keeps it for himself. brigitte's mother had to learn that. her glitter came from a sales rep. when did it fade? many years ago. with his company car.

brigitte's mother says, brigitte should keep heinz on a loose rein, but not let go, not yet lock him up, only lock him up later, but nevertheless keep a firm hold on him, bind him to her, with a thousand little things, for example with a little baby. but also with special manual talents and skills: e.g. doing the laundry.

evidently brigitte's mother has still not had enough. evidently there is still a little free space in brigitte's mother's big mouth.

it is a merciless hunt.

neither hunted heinz, nor the poor weary hunter brigitte, are granted a rest during its course. sometimes the hunter can be in a worse situation than the game.

in brigitte's case she's in worse state than he is.

susi is a glittering person. bathed in sunlight susi leaps playfully at a lemon-coloured butterfly, a brimstone. her blonde hair is just like blonde hair.

for some the sunlight is enough to give a shine, others again need a whole electrician's shop.

b. should not be so immodest and be satisfied with the sun, like susi.

susi is bathed in the sun in the garden. the garden does not belong to her, but to heinz, therefore to brigitte. b. chases after susi and throws her to the ground, out of range of any possible glitter. most of all she'd like to bury susi in the ground, in the damp loam.

panting brigitte lies spreadeagled on top of susi and explains, why one can do what one likes with one's own property, but can only do with others' property, what the owner of the other property, in this case brigitte, permits. an example: in the factory, says b., i have to do what i'm told. but in my metal locker, i can do what I like, because it's MINE, it can be tidy or untidy, whatever i like. tidy of course. in the canteen i have to be friendly, because the canteen is shared by everyone, but at my place at table, i can do what i like. it is MINE alone. yes, it's the little things that count.

and she dunks susi's head in a puddle, until heinz comes, and pulls susi out of her hands again.

and, if the owner of our factory came to my home, b. continues, then there even he would have to do what i want, because my home is my castle. as small as it is, there nevertheless i can give the orders.

your factory owner will never come to your house, because you are so unfriendly, susi mumbles to herself.

never? perhaps he will come one day after all. and no one could stop him, not even you, who want to prevent so many things. you couldn't intimidate my factory owner.

perhaps one day he'll come and visit me as well as my mother!

he'll never come, retorts susi: because you are unimportant. because you are the lowest and most unimportant thing there is.

but IF he did come, in our apartment he would HAVE to do what we say, that's even the legal law, sobs brigitte. she knows better.

five minutes later the two fighting cocks are sitting having a snack.

brigitte had said interesting things, much of it specu-
lation, just as it is in the world of business.
perhaps brigitte will be able to make use of the results
of this conversation, one day when she has her own
shop and heinz.

so now love is there

so now love has already come x-times, but a better
life has still not begun for paula. it's time that life and
development at last entered this muddled situation.
paula cannot enjoy her great love properly at all,
because she has to get up at five and make breakfast
for her dadda. paula knows, that a great love needs
time, in order to grow, so that it grows even bigger.
paula has no time.
at the same time paula's momma climbs up the
mountain pasture with the rake, in order to cultivate
her little kingdom. momma continuously surveys her
kingdom, from one housewife's border to the next.
momma's head jerks from side to side, searching for
illegal border crossings.
momma continuously looks from one end of her
kingdom to the other, back and forward, she's happy,
that she has a housewife's kingdom.
others perhaps have more, others perhaps are car-
penters, electricians, plumbers, bricklayers, watch-
makers, butchers! or pork butchers!
but at least everyone in the family is healthy.
when momma has a bad day, then she thinks, that
the pork butcher's wife for example has a housewife's
kingdom of her own, but also a smokeroom of her
own. then momma gives her little grandson franzi a

shove with the sharp toothed rake. franzi's bawling and bellowing compensates momma for the pork butcher's wife having two kingdoms, a housewife's kingdom and a pork butcher's wife's kingdom. franzi's cries guide momma back to the heart of the matter, that is, to the fact that she herself has everything a woman can wish for. and everyone is healthy. the pork butcher's wife is forgotten. franzi is comforted at length. what more can a momma wish for? nothing.

paula's momma can wish for nothing more, because she has already consumed her fate, without anything coming of it.

so since paula's momma can wish for nothing more, because it's too late, she is perfectly happy.

perfectly happy momma goes out into the fields. she eavesdrops on herself, in case somewhere deep inside a melody rings out or a blackbird sings, but all that she hears, is only the cancer, which saws and eats away at her. momma doesn't even have alcohol as an antidote to cancer.

the cancer too has seen prettier sights than this ruined womb, in which in the course of the long years of marriage a thing or two has happened. we don't even want to mention the abortion sessions in boiling hot water.

what the doctor was never allowed to see, that is now left to this dangerous fatal illness. it almost looks, as if one had virtually spent one's whole life saving up the last tiny energies, in order then to be killed, to be ravaged slowly and painfully.

for whom then in the end did dadda ravage this womb? for the illness. the illness harvests, what can still be harvested. there's not much left.

momma it is true has already read a lot about this pernicious illness in the weekend papers, nevertheless fear strikes her now with full force. although she has read, that fear only makes everything worse and one should keep one's balance, she is terribly afraid and loses her balance completely.

one day paula said, that she would go to the gynaecologist, to get the pill prescribed, when the time came, so that one doesn't have so many children. you cow, says her little mother then, letting a strange man prod about inside you, disgusting. paula won't do that as long as she's living in her housewife's kingdom.

paula is reassured, because she is not going to live in her momma's kingdom much longer, but soon in her own kingdom.

but erich is not yet making any move to do anything at all.

dressmaking is now making paula really nervous and restless. the journeys to the county town to her employer and teacher are only distractions from erich. paula can hardly wait to come home again. a pity that we won't get any data from the paula experiment. paula would like to withdraw into private life. goodbye, paula, on a more private, cosier level!

hardly is paula back from her dressmaking apprenticeship, than she throws on her best red dress and marches up the mountain, to erich. at the top paula is then intercepted like a boomerang, before she has even properly recovered from the momentum, turned round, a kick in the arse, and the girl rushes home.

paula runs up the mountain, is turned round on her

axis, and races down again, like a fire alarm. in vain as it were.

up there erich's momma and erich's grandmomma give the orders. it's the only man in the house who really gives the orders, erich's stepdada, who is a retired civil servant, which not many can say of themselves, when the day of reckoning finally comes.

asthma, the stepdada, so-called because he is an asthmatic, makes the two decrepit females obey, its a joy to see.

for asthma it's a joy. for the two women it's less of a joy, but a joy nevertheless.

he does it in a subtle way, the civil servant's way.

he does it without saying a word, by his personality alone. asthma, the sick pensioner, sits like a toad on its spot and is provided with food, drink and the tv programmes.

rattling nastily inside, asthma hovers over everything like a bad dream.

asthma has everything completely under control, just as once he had a small but very important part of the federal railways under his control. asthma often talks about those days. then an atmosphere of breathless excitement prevails.

while asthma, interrupted by the rattle in his throat, provides entertainment with his unbelievable but true anecdotes from a railwayman's life, momma scrubs and cleans into him and out of him again, over his head and under his feet, it's a pleasure to see.

momma has felt no trace of pleasure for years.

the pleasure, which momma sometimes felt long ago, she had to pay for dearly, with a whole swarm of children.

because pleasure was followed by a more durable joy, a joy, that was not so exciting, but all the more lasting: the joy of having children.

asthma lets himself be tended with pleasure like a leghorn hen.

asthma would like momma to erase every memory of earlier joys in herself. best of all he would like to see her scratch the dirt from the floor with her fingernails. unfortunately only momma's death will be able to erase all the unclean things she once did.

asthma keeps his wife, who in the past very often stumbled, under strict supervision. asthma and his wife are certainly on the right path, they are almost in the grave. only a little while longer.

in the peaceful mountain atmosphere asthma watches his wife as she works. momma's bad hip cracks in protest at this rough treatment. it does her no good. someone has to do it after all, and this someone is momma. gratitude helps her as she does it.

gratitude wrings out a wet rag for her.

the rheumatic fever is glad of that.

momma is like an empty bean pod or like an empty shopping net, which everything fell out of long ago. like a net which is torn as well.

paula meanwhile runs up the hill.

when the postbus sounds its horn, it's also a sign for erich's momma, that paula is back from work.

momma's already waiting up at the top of the hill, aha, now paula is putting on fresh underwear, now she's combing her few mousey hairs, now she's picking up the lipstick and now the plastic shoes, which were cheap, but are elegant. now the little bag as well, in matching white. now: ready, march!

to erich.

now momma gets going too, easy does it, don't rush, is the watchword today.

there paula is already emerging behind the bend, surging against the stubborn and sour old woman. if it's about the man, it's all right, if it's about work, suddenly it's not all right, thinks momma sour and eaten up with hate.

paula runs against erich's momma, as a bird flies against a window pane, against a concrete wall, the effect is the same: no further.

ready, march. downhill, in the opposite direction, and put a bit of swing into it please.

momma says, that paula has no business here. and that although paula has left her heart here!

momma wants erich to go on attending to the single cow, which provides milk for dada's coffee, and that in addition he feeds the pig. momma has tb of the bones, which is a hard fate, which erich must make easier for her. after the life she led momma had deserved something worse than tb, but got a civil servant. paula deserves something much much worse, and she'll get it too.

erich is needed for the rough work and for the light, to the extent that his brain is up to it.

good evening, i'm coming to see erich, paula just manages to chirrup, but no more than that. she should be ashamed of herself, running after erich. erich is the productive property of all of them.

like a wind up toy animal paula whizzes down the hill again, each step takes her further from her goal, erich.

when she happens not to be working, momma constantly sits at her lookout window looking down to the pass and sniffing the air.

when she's not working, paula constantly sits down at the bottom of the path looking up to the pass and sniffing the air.

and grandmomma sits at the lookout in her room, grandmomma is so old, that she is merely tolerated and would be quite lost without her daughter and the daughter maintaining son-in-law asthma. grand-momma's existence hangs by a silken thread, because one mouth more is one mouth too many, if asthma eats almost everything by himself.

grandmomma and momma keep watch in shifts, so that no one takes their erich away from them. no one will take asthma away anyhow, he'll be left to them. so now not only do they all hate each other, now in fine unanimity they all hate paula as well, who only has love as well as herself to give away.

which is too little.

paula would certainly exploit erich's labour power for her own dirty goals, for a little house, for a little child, a couple of little children and a car. the benefit, which paula would have from erich, cannot at all be outweighed by erich's thrashings of paula. blows never outweigh money. money is heavier than blows.

paula however has only herself and her love to give away.

which is too little.

the differences between susi and brigitte
what susi and brigitte possibly have in
common

there is an immovable demarcation line between susi
and brigitte: the full coffee pot. it is a sharp painful
division, which puts each in her place, which sepa-
rates the two incompatible characters. when however
one of them lifts the pot and pours out coffee, then
suddenly susi and brigitte are together and not
separate.

a dividing point for example is that susi would like
to achieve good for all mankind, for everyone, big or
small, but especially for the starving little babies in
the whole world, because she is a woman and will
soon be a mother. starving babies are a dreadful
thought to susi, the woman in her is outraged at it,
the future mother in her rebels against it.

for this reason and for this purpose she is even a little
involved in a political school students' group and
very much involved in a folk dance group. the political school students' group she skilfully hides from
her dear parents, the folk dance group she bears
before her like a cock pigeon his hen.

brigitte wants heinz. for susi debating and discussing
come first. many words and the objects which go
with them occur to her, she lets them out again the
moment they occur.

every time she opens her mouth susi brings up a
whole portion of starving people throughout the
world. brigitte saves the whipped cream from susi's
discharge. susi also likes to learn cooking, which one
learns in her girls' grammar school, so that one day,
when susi is married, her spouse and children at least

will not need to starve like many others, whom susi could mention. susi has very many different expressions for hunger and injustice. for brigitte the only injustice is, that heinz bothers with susi. for susi it is an injustice, that heinz is full up and satisfied, while many starve. she says further, that it is nice to dance folk dances in a folk dance group, but that it is also nice, precisely as a contrast to folk dancing, if one is a thinking person, who worries about the misery in the world.

brigitte knows only a single word: heinz. it is true she knows the word for work, but never says it out loud, because she doesn't relate to it. she says very proudly, that she is never hungry and never will be hungry unlike many others, whom she couldn't mention, but who no doubt get what they deserve, because hunger is unnecessary, if one works hard, at which b. thinks of heinz and his hard work, but not of her own hard work.

b. boasts that she always has enough, and that one day heinz will even have more than enough, so much, that there will even be more than enough for both of them.

sometimes brigitte has enough of everything. sometimes she has it up to here. but when she looks at heinz at such moments, then suddenly she has far too little, then heinz should go into action, start up his engine, and put in some work.

some work, of which everyone can see the result.

heinz has a talent for technical things, therefore the work he does must be in the area of technology. susi and brigitte are proud of what technology creates every day. brigitte is prouder than susi, because heinz is one of those who have submitted to technology, who know how to handle it. heinz and brigitte will sell many electrical appliances, heinz will even be able to repair them.

susi is prouder than brigitte, because she will be able to afford any number of these appliances. she will then be able to tell heinz, what he has to repair, if any of them is broken.

there is a big difference between brigitte's craft pride and susi's owner's pride. brigitte is not a skilled worker, heinz is the skilled worker. heinz is proud too.

heinz is proud, because one day he can take on skilled workers, who will carry out the dirty repair jobs for him. heinz will then only supervise the business.

meanwhile susi still feels sorry for people, who are worse off than she is.

meanwhile brigitte is still not sorry for anyone at all, because she has to concentrate entirely on heinz.

susi isn't interested in heinz. evidently susi already has everything.

susi also feels sorry for brigitte.

brigitte feels sorry for susi, because susi is unable to recognise heinz's qualities.

nevertheless, although she doesn't want to draw susi's attention to these qualities, although she doesn't want to make susi's mouth water, brigitte talks about nothing else except heinz's qualities.

susi still feels sorry for brigitte, who doesn't seem to understand, that there are better quality products than heinz.

it's noticeable, that there is a natural boundary between the two of them, which is so firm, that it cannot be torn down.

brigitte is more susi's enemy than susi is brigitte's enemy.

heinz listens attentively to what susi is explaining.

he looks around and all around to find somewhere the hunger of which there is supposed to be so much. then for a joke he says, all this talk about hunger and starvation has really given me an appetite for a schnitzel.

grunting heinz strokes his potbelly.

susi and brigitte leap up as if bitten by two tarantulas. each tries to overtake the other on the way to the kitchen. susi out of pride, brigitte out of fear of what susi can do.

the two girls fall on top of one another squealing. they beat each other black and blue. brigitte's skin is even grazed. heinz lies in the deck chair and enjoys the silence and nature and the smells from the kitchen. now he really has an appetite for a nice wiener schnitzel with cucumber salad.

good-humouredly he listens to brigitte's cursing and bawling. she would like to pull susi away from the kitchen stove by the hair. she doesn't succeed however, because susi has trained for athletics and also plays tennis and basketball. brigitte gets rapped across the knuckles. brigitte howls. she cries like a jackal, all her enjoyment of a nice day dissolves in the sizzling fat. meanwhile susi gets to work.

susi is as calm and ice cold and deliberate as death itself, while she beats the eggs.

mother too eavesdrops on the goings-on in the kitchen with mixed feelings. daddy says, why do these girls always have to cackle like hens. one half of her says, that now she'll lose her heinz to susi. she raised him, now susi will get him, who will be good for him however and take care of his stomach, no problem. mother's other half says, now brigitte will not get a look-in.

quite apart from the old people's home heinz's momma will not be right about that. heinz thinks, that susi will soon no longer give a shit about world hunger, when she has to devote herself entirely to *his* hunger. susi's day will then be filled up more completely.

susi will get his cock firmly inserted in her snatch and family life firmly inserted in her head.

heinz holds the reins firmly in his hand.

so, the schnitzels are cooked through.

susi has done them. for that susi is allowed to carry everything in. brigitte tries to knock it out of her hand, but heinz's mother is faster and raps her knuckles so hard that it echoes.

i want to have peace and quiet when i'm eating, says heinz complacently to the bawling brigitte. be quiet, otherwise you'll get one from me too. better safe than sorry.

better safe than sorry. brigitte falls silent immediately, she thinks about her two-fold happiness, about the house and about the shop for electrical appliances. brigitte is silent, so as not to put her future at risk.

susi is quite swollen up with pride. she has very clean and pure thoughts.

heinz the fat pig has very unclean thoughts, which are now however pushed into the background by food. although susi always skilfully conceals the fact that she has something between her legs, there must be something there, but what. after the cake and the coffee, when heinz is full up, he'll think about susi's pussy.

now heinz is not thinking about anything at all, his jaws grind slowly but surely.

brigitte is so eaten up with hate, that she cannot eat anything herself. she tries to disparage susi's schnitzel. heinz praises it instead. he right away consumes brigitte's portion too. that's how good it tasted.

heinz considers himself to be the germ of the primordial cell, so his dear parents have taught him.

heinz believes, that he and a thoroughbred woman like susi would make the ideal union.

susi it is true believes, that she is a thoroughbred woman, but not that there could be any kind of union with heinz. susi wants a thoroughbred for a husband, which heinz is not. to susi heinz is a greedy prole. to susi, susi is an excellent cook, to her father also.

susi tries, to further explain the misery all around, and to arouse heinz's family against this misery.

heinz's father says in a very friendly way, she should shut her trap, because his son heinz doesn't like to hear anything sad while he is eating, only something cheerful. and now his son happens to be at his food again, can susi not see that.

shocked, susi falls silent, she is ashamed for the indifferent public which is here personified in heinz's father. susi is quiet and begins to dream: another two hours gone, and still no senior consultant in sight.

heinz goes on dreaming about little things: little susi in a little skirt in his kitchen.

you'll soon forget all that when you're married, jokes heinz, the expert, the specialist, wise to the ways of the world, who knows it all from his parents. heinz, who always talks in generalities, as if he knew it all, had learned it, or had the experience. and yet he has only learned it from his parents and his workmates. his parents don't know anything themselves, otherwise his daddy wouldn't be a van driver. otherwise, however, his mummy would still have to go on doing the housekeeping. no matter what the husband is, the housekeeping remains to one. heinz talks, as if he has great experience of life, which he doesn't have.

susi talks about her hobbies: foreign people and places. heinz the expert says, there's no place like home. susi is scornful. heinz knows better anyway, heinz, the man's man. brigitte meanwhile demonstrates how careful she is with heinz's family's china and little spoons.

brigitte protects the china against damage by outsiders.

she demonstrates, how much she likes the china set with the little flowers, she holds the cups in her fingers like a newborn chick. very carefully. one would never expect it of these unskilled hands. heinz's parents are embarrassed. perhaps susi will think that china is something special for heinz's family, whereas it's only something special for b. the worker. heinz's parents hurriedly protest that they eat off china with little flowers every day, if a piece gets broken, well, then one just buys a new piece instead.

brigitte believes, that with so much loving care the foreign thoughts, which she sometimes notices in heinz now, must disappear, which they do not, because they are native thoughts inherited from his parents. brigitte's mistake.

susi simply grabs the pot, as if it were made of tin

and already belonged to her. but we're not in prison drinking out of tin mugs, but drinking out of china cups with the family of my future fiancé. fiancé! brigitte wants to take the pot away from her, protect it and press it to her heart and rock it like a baby, so that everyone sees, how much she appreciates what will soon belong to her. his parents should shut their mouths, they can eat from a tin plate in the old people's home, the doddery old fools.

one of the two girls is seriously mistaken. brigitte as always. brigitte and susi try to look sweet and feminine.

susi is successful at it, because she really is sweet, which is easy for her, since it doesn't cost anything and makes everyone around her happy. even if it cost something, susi could still afford it.

brigitte is unsuccessful at it, because on the hard road to heinz she herself has become hard and embittered. with brigitte it must not cost anything, only her substance. quite a few uninvited guests are already eating at brigitte's substance: the obstinate brassière line is the most unwelcome of all. brigitte's substance is thin as worn silk.

only tenacity still holds the fort. love has long since gone to sleep. no one can stay up so late.

once again love had to fail and brutality win.

susi always has to win, because she is so sweet and good. because she is human. brigitte is inhuman.

with brute force, brigitte wins the battle for the coffee pot. susi, who is soft and feminine, has to let the pot go. brigitte, who is hard and unfeminine, triumphantly seizes the pot, the pot is at brigitte's breast: victory. susi says we've got a much nicer one at home, that's where i'm going now.

heinz's mother throws herself in susi's way, so that she stays longer. she promises, that she will buy the most beautiful pot there is, if only susi stays. she draws susi to her breast, which years ago suckled heinz and later made him a man who keeps his eyes on what's essential. and not on what's inessential – brigitte.

heinz's mother says to susi, they should femininely stick together against unfeminine hardness – brigitte.

in the end susi has won the battle, thanks to her femininity and softness. just stay that way, susi! don't let yourself be hardened!

more than anything heinz would like to box brigitte's ears. the next moment heinz boxes brigitte's ears anyway. a man must do, what he has made up his mind to do. this injustice hurts! after all, brigitte saved the family pot from an intruder. she still presses the china to her, the china is already warm as a human body, unlike heinz, who is always cold to b.

there is a large brown stain on the table cloth. susi races into the kitchen, to make room for her instincts, which are telling her: clean the table cloth!

the wet cloth appears in the picture. it's a beautiful personal success for susi as the cloth slides over the table. i'll only give the pot to mother-in-law or heinz, but not to you, says brigitte. but no one bothers about her. an enthusiastic crowd, consisting of heinz and his parents, applauds susi.

brigitte does not exist. if she were not still holding the pot in her insect-bitten paws, no one would see her at all.

what brigitte did wrong with her lack of femininity, susi has put right again.

she won't accept any thanks, no no.
brigitte wants heinz.
she won't get him like *that* at any rate.

where there's a love, there's a way

the priest says, that love is a way to the self. paula is looking for an understanding with erich. paula is therefore looking for a more earthly way to the self. paula is looking for a basis, on which she can meet erich, so that they can then carry on their dirty business together.

every system, no matter how rigid, has a loophole somewhere one can slip through. love often consists of discovering such loopholes. paula's love right away thought of the co-op shop. her future momma-in-law has forgotten the co-op shop, in which erich always has to do the big weekend shopping. he is given a little book, in which everything is written down. erich gives what's been written down to the branch manager, who arranges the things for him in the rucksack, which slowly becomes heavier and leans over towards the inn.

everywhere around erich and almost into erich stand walls made of women's bodies, nothing but mommas, at least one momma of every age, in front of the shop the fruits of their wombs crowd together by the dozen, hang in thick bunches at the door, crash their scooters into buses, cars and wagons piled with wood, get trapped under motor bikes, station wagons and trucks with trailers, more rarely under the slower tractors, in front of which one can still jump to the side. a natural wastage is noticeable and ascertainable among these fruits of the womb. but that doesn't matter, because new ones can always be made, if some drop out. the making is already not very pleasant, carrying them probably even less so, giving birth is certainly no fun, and having them brings one down. but all the same: existence as a mother is justified and assured for another couple of years.

everyone can see: that is a complete family. the husband can see: now i have yet another creature apart from my wife, whom i can thrash and bawl at, children's flesh is soft, but the surface is small.

the wife can see: i've certainly achieved something, that should be an incentive to me, to achieve something more.

the little child itself: the central figure, the living justification for all uselessly wasted time, for a time, which is bursting at the seams with useless activities, activities which are never carried out for oneself, always only for others, with the dubious thought at the back of the mind, that in the end they will be reflected back again as glorious light at least in the sunday sermon, which never happens, because it is true the activities fall back on one, but not as a halo, rather as a hundredweight, which in the end crushes one to pulp. and one day a shapeless mass called mama goes to bed for the last time with someone called papa who was buried a long time ago.

the central figure however, the little child, is swaddled and coddled, till it can walk and go on its scooter, then its ears are boxed, it's loaded with shopping bags, mown down by scythes, squashed under cars, or it falls into the torrent, into the hands of the drunk father, gets in the way of the chopping of firewood or into some molester's hands. if one survives all that, one can still, drunk at 15, crash into the concrete bridge pier on the moped.

often one can observe a child engaged in a weakly quivering attempt at play, from which it is immediately dragged away, plied with clouts around the ear and supplied with kicks, then with the rucksack, and off to buy animal feed. bran and salt.

our paula foresees nothing of this, as outside the co-op door, she distributes sweeties under the suspicious looks of the mothers and hoping for erich's admiring eyes. all the bigger children are not allowed to eat their sweeties, but must take them home for their little infant or toddler brothers and sisters. if they do nevertheless stick one in their mouths, they get hit so hard, their teeth wobble.

again and again the boiling saucepan is abandoned here and the woman hurls herself like a fury at the weak-willed baby, to tug the shitty garment from its body and with wild energy to clap a snow white freshly washed covering around the silly little thing. then numerous kisses from numerous mouths are pressed against the stuffed little romper suits. removal of the crap to the washing machine. how the nasty smelly brown stuff is replaced by something, that is even whiter than white is a constantly repeated ever fresh miracle of nature. the crap is forgotten, the sun shines again. many mouths, which happen to be on an admiring visit, then say you little piggy-wiggy to the little child and you hard working mummy to the happy mother.

paula often has an urge to see erich. mummy often has an urge to clean things.

there he is already: erich the urge. the smart young

man looks especially attractive against this background of women's bodies, doddery pensioners and
too heavily laden minors. erich parts the apathetic
scene like a curtain and is there.

unwed women in squeaky white coats tense behind
the shop counter, among them an unmarried
mother, the lad will end up in the forest soon too.
perms, new dept. store jumpers under the coat, flat
laced shoes with fat white calves above them, gold
teeth and gold chains with a little cross. many difficult questions about his momma, his grandmomma
and his dada rain down on erich, erich's replies come
much more slowly than the questions. erich stands
before the questions like a bull before a gate. well,
thank you. his eyes, which otherwise are always
allowed to enjoy the fresh country air, are not used
to the neon light. the neon light is unnatural and
unhealthy. erich is as good-looking as he is tall.

the sales assistants immediately get a longing for a
little love.

erich has not only little, but no love at all to give
away. not even his closest relatives, who have more
than once sprained their hands for him and his thrashings, can count on it, on erich's love. erich would
very much like to strike his dada and his momma
dead, which he doesn't dare do however. it's nice
instead, to torment a little dog, a cat or a small child,
when no one's looking.

if paula knew that.

paula is out for love like a pig out for acorns.

paula snuffles in every crack for erich, to make him
a present of her body.

the whole inn sits back and watches this activity in

silence, but will soon actively intervene in the battle of the sexes.

when one is drunk, it is true that one gives out thrashings more readily than when one is not drunk, but one gets less out of it, because one carries it out as if in a fog and does not even remember it properly. erich still has to find a happy medium, but he's got years left for that, until senility or the tree falls down on top of him. many years of practice.

paula still believes, that life and love lie before her, she still does not know that at most her own love alone lies before her. one has to do everything oneself. but then at least something will come of it. if one does it oneself, then at least it's done properly, one can't really rely on anyone any more.

brakes squeal outside. one at least has got away.

paula escorts erich together with his purchases into the old barn. a crowd of healthy country children have entered there before her and come out again sick. some indeed have found happiness there and subsequently lost it again, most have found misfortune there. few have found something there, that was fun. a feeling of happiness is not the rule, here calculations, additions, and subtractions prevail. it is icy cold.

here much has not been fulfilled, which had been expected. here not a few have said, soon we shall be three. here many a marriage and many a heart has been broken. here passion prevails, which however no one has yet set eyes on. here one enters as an emotional cripple and leaves again as an emotional cripple. what was in between, is nothing at all, changes nothing. here the law of the genitals prevails, in contrast to the law of the forest, which applies at work. afterwards a number of different solutions of tide swallow the various soiled underpants, which marched into the barn freshly washed.

erich stumbles a little under the heavy rucksack and under the influence of master alcohol. paula has pains in her chest and has difficulty breathing, because she is expecting something big. big erich is already there, nothing bigger can follow that.

paula was very much looking forward to love, which she doesn't get however. long after erich has gone again paula is still looking for love between the posts, in the battered manger, in the hay and in the dung channel.

but paula's snatch hurts, that's all.

and erich climbs up the mountain – trala!

paula has been informed that love hurts when there's a loss, an accident involving a sports car, a death under the surgeon's knife or a tragic suicide.

so how is it possible, that love hurts, when it comes? not only when it goes?

paula sits in the hay and wipes away the blood with a sunday handkerchief. almost in an instant the desired child in her brain has turned into a terrible fear and an acute threat. from wanted child to feared child. now paula has to face the consequences.

if paula couldn't even hold on to erich for more than two minutes with her underdeveloped body, her meagre mind, the dressmaking she's begun and her new red dress, how would she be able to hold on to erich with a little child?

we have not described the love between erich and paula, because it wasn't there. it was like a hole into which one stumbles, and after which one hobbles

away again. nothing is broken, except a human creature in the bloom of her youth.

washday at home also swallows without difficulty the
red handkerchief. just as it has swallowed dada's and
bruda's sweaty workshirts. joy, sorrow and work all
lie so close to one another.

it's hard work for paula to get erich and keep him.
now love is no longer in the genitals, but only in the
head. the genitals are numb and feel nothing any
more.

that way the genitals save themselves a lot of bother.
better a gleaming new kitchen than a bit of pleasure
below the belt. pleasure passes, but the kitchen
endures.

there must be a washing machine too.

paula must now combine the performance of a
machine with the skill of a tightrope walker.

what threatens her, is more than a fall.

what threatens her, is the absence of her monthly
trouble.

and it's not always nice, if a trouble is absent.

unfortunately

there are not only garden weekends, thinks brigitte,
after duty has just called: brigitte, come!

many enter work as unchanged people and come out
again as hardened people changed for the worse.

brigitte does not want to be hardened, she wants to
be impregnated.

in brigitte's head there is nothing but heinz.

heinz is at the end of a long swamp similar to the
one which can be found in the heads of many of her

workmates. only, there is not a heinz sitting and waving at the end of every swamp, also no nickel-plated bathtaps, no bathroom fittings, boiler, hot water tank and lavatory bowl.

at the end of the many other swamps wait people, who are mentally, physically and in character far below heinz.

often they have no sense of duty.

brigitte has no sense of duty either. in marriage brigitte will learn a sense of duty as many young women before her, who previously had been fairly easy-going and relaxed, have already done.

heinz exists – out of a sense of duty to his body's need for relaxation and to his friends – to play skittles. b. goes along to play skittles out of mistrust and suspicion of heinz. often heinz sees other women at skittles, sometimes even ones without rightful owners.

stray women are very dangerous for a young immature man like heinz, who has first to be made mature in marriage.

when brigitte has her heinz whole and in one piece in bed afterwards, so that the stench of beer sprays in all directions, then she has such a sincere feeling of gratitude, that her frogs' legs open of their own accord as if moved by magic.

admittedly she still feels nothing, but the tremendous relief allows brigitte to relax.

which is necessary, because she has another hard working day in front of her.

so it has

so it has indeed failed to appear in paula.

after the fear of the absence of her monthly trouble, which no woman in paula's surroundings could think of as other than a trouble, the absence has now indeed inexorably followed.

until now nothing has come of love yet, now something has failed to appear, which announces that something will come, which will activate paula's function. something BIG.

the breath of life and/or erich's cock has brushed paula and not only brushed.

dressmaking is still there, only erich is never there.

paula is not allowed to go up the mountain, which makes no difference to her, because the forthcoming happy event, as it's called, envelops her in the valley too.

paula's forthcoming happy event must first of all be confided in the man, whom she loves and who loves her, so that the wedding can follow.

soon the forthcoming event will make paula's face softer, her glance more affectionate, her stomach fatter, her breasts heavier, her back more painful and her trousers wetter. reason: paula is shit scared of her parents, who are rough, but has a secret, which is sweet.

paula has still not said i love you to erich, because she hardly knows him, now she can kill two birds with one stone: i love you, and i'm expecting your child.

paula must also inform her momma and her dada. oh dear.

paula particularly needs erich at this time of anticipation, because it is a crisis situation for every woman and a burden for every female organism, but a joyful one. at this time of hope especially paula needs understanding, care and protection from wild animals, rough work, hard blows and inhuman treatment. on every occasion of inhuman treatment, no matter how small, paula thinks, you would feel sorry, if you knew, that i feel an emergent life in me. the unborn life in paula is straining towards the sun.

in unhealthy nightmares paula sometimes imagines, what would happen, if she said to her dada: daddy, i need a great deal of care and attention especially now, because something unborn in me is straining and stretching towards the sun. then an iron hand of terror grips paula. although her daddy himself made children again and again.

will he say, hurrah, that's my grandchild just coming out of my daughter, welcome, walk right in! and now we have a young, just born baby life in our household again, the main thing is, that it's happy?

and momma, will she deliver a specialist expert report on this happy, long but not endless condition? will she surround her daughter with care and maintenance? will she help in procuring the baby outfit? blue or pink? or yellow? it's fun. for then not only paula, but also a second life will be living a good life. two happy lives at once instead of solitary dressmaking.

and erich, the happy father, will spend every free minute with mother and child, will spend every free minute looking after his young wife, give up alcohol, no longer hate anybody, not fritter away any money any more and so forth.

paula intends, to open her whole overburdened heart

to her momma. the reason: her momma has herself
been several times a momma and consequently
understands this condition, which paula is in. she
even understands this condition better than a man,
who can always only be a daddy and has nothing
more to do with all that shit, that's women's business.
paula tells women's business to a woman, that is her
momma, who is a woman.

paula places trust in the femininity of her mother,
which is disappointed.

momma sharpens paula and hammers her straight
into the ground. and every child which ever in times
past weighed down a mother's stomach, seems to be
hammering busily with her, so much strength is there
in the woman all at once.

until now paula has only heard axe blows echo so
loud in the forest. it would be merry work, bashing
paula, if it were not carried out with so much hate.
love unites, but hate divides. paula's momma hates
paula because of the child in her stomach. various
of paula's important organs break under this treatment.

paula's momma has often enough hated her husband
because of the children in her stomach, because of
the extra work and the horrible birth process, has
also very many times hated the children inside her
stomach and later the children outside her stomach,
now momma has finally cracked, so that she not only
hates a child outside her stomach in her daughter's
stomach, but the daughter as well. people will think
that one hasn't brought up one's own daughter properly. what a scandal and a mockery. on top of this
insane amount of work scandal and mockery every
day as well. without further ado paula's momma

could list over a dozen people, all woodcutters plus family, who would gloat with pleasure over her misfortune, equally without further ado.

in part people in whose misfortune (feeble-minded son, father inside for child molesting, momma's womb cleaned out, dada killed by falling tree, momma run away and working in the factory, child repeating at school for the second time, loss of driving licence for drunkenness, climbing accident in the mountains, brand new chair chopped up by son etc.) one had oneself once taken enormous pleasure.

possibly these cretins will now take all the more pleasure in one's own calamity, which is a hideous idea.

paula's expecting a child.

paula's expecting a child!

oh there is a merry hating in the bottom of this valley.

hate spreads like wildfire from one mountain to the next.

and paula right in the middle of it, perhaps even the cause.

paula comes tiptoeing sweetly to her likewise momma, puts her uncombed little head under the latter's arm, just as little paula always used to do in unhappy childhood times, comes very sweetly to confess and wants a couple of knitting and/or crochet tips for the sweet little blue or pink jacket, that she wants to knit, make or crochet for erich's offspring.

as usual paula's trust is rewarded with terrible thrashings and loud cries of hate.

paula's head only hangs by a thread, there is hardly an unmarked spot on her expectant mother's body.

and just wait till her strong father appears in the picture, which we call reality!

here he comes already, hears the news in telegram style, no precious thrashing time to be lost, momma is still quite breathless from thrashing paula, she doesn't even get the story out properly and with all the causes and connections. she has to hit and hit again.

and so it goes on, a hunting they do go, no better time, who was the swine, who is the swine, which swine must marry now, whether he will or not?

a wonder, that no miscarriage follows this exciting day.

erich with the pig's head.

paula isn't up to as much as usual after that. paula hasn't ever been up to much. people say that mental wounds often hurt more than physical ones, but in this case paula's physical wounds are no laughing matter either, they need much care and not a few poultices.

paula feels that she is being treated as unpleasant object and not as the human being that she is. if her parents had laid into a hard, unyielding object, they would probably even have cracked a wrist.

one doesn't need to waste any words here on paula's state of mind. she has become a rock hard, numbed person.

and no erich comes to her aid. erich belongs to the forest, but the forest by no means belongs to erich.

so no talk woman to woman. the cut out crochet patterns lie crumpled, dirty and soiled on the floor.

paula is admittedly unsoiled, but nevertheless without hope. the child in the tight belly is threatened by the popular and trusted soapy bath, which should make a little angel of it, but sometimes doesn't work, because the growing life clings too tightly to the womb.

good boiling hot soap suds out of good clean brightly coloured detergent packets with lots of good poison in them. that would even kill dada, if he ate it. dada however prefers woodcutter's sausage.

a negotiator is on the way to erich through forests, fields and mountain streams. the situation is far from romantic.

by the time of the wedding the abrasions, cuts and bruises will hopefully have faded away.

a song sings in paula, but very faintly.

instead of wounds a white lace dress down to the ground plus veil.

no soap suds, but a nice flowered bonnet.

no abortion, but a good wedding cake.

no dead little embryo, but a good pork joint.

the looks of hate stare out of the kitchen like thorns, so many thorns, that one can hardly enter the kitchen.

many disappointed lives and hopes now take simultaneous revenge on paula.

the last remnant of enjoyment of life in paula dribbles away into the ground. there is a complete absence of physical sensation.

the attempt to kill off little susanne in paula's stomach does not succeed. dada and momma were successfully killed off years ago. for paula a world has caved in, which makes no difference, because not a single little piece of it ever belonged to paula.

i even have a friend

i have a girlfriend, who's at college, brigitte brags to a secretary and her canary islands. at the thought of susi, the natural enemy, brigitte's stomach contracts, the filter coffee in her almost overflows and comes pouring back out of mouth and nostrils. right away brigitte hopes that this time it's worked and she's pregnant. but it was only the susi in her.

brigitte brags, that susi treats her like a person.

with possessive gestures the secretary moves various office objects just a little. she feels affiliated to her boss, she does not for a single second feel affiliated to brigitte. there is a yawning gulf between brigitte and her. the gulf between brigitte and her is called secretarial college.

there is nothing more to be said, only to be felt.

there is nothing more to be done except wait.

brigitte and paula are waiting for marriage.

heinz is a good man, because he will marry brigitte because of her child and establish a life for her in the world of business.

here one can neither pass the time of waiting with music, nor with a good thriller, nor with a tv pro-gramme, nor with a skittles evening. the time of wait-ing would have to be a time of empty pages. erich is not such a good man, because he doesn't want to marry paula because of the child. he has to never-theless.

yet again heinz's father, the loser, holds his son down in a stranglehold and the worn out discs do their bit too. they tap messages of pain up to the father's brain. the father speaks with the force of his whole desolate experience of life. heinz pants for air and susi.

susi pants for air in the firm athletic embraces of her athletic father, who can also play tennis. susi's father embraces his daughter, because she has managed a whole gateau by herself.

heinz's father has not quite managed to reach the end of his life yet, although his ruined back will hardly manage anything useful any more, either for his master and employer nor for the father himself. heinz still has his life in front of him, so he believes.

brigitte has heinz's life in front of her.

so while his father holds heinz in a stranglehold, with all the unused energies of a van driver no longer suited to van driving, his mother kneels on heinz's chest and implores heinz not to rob them of the fruits of their thriftiness, by bringing someone like brigitte into the home they've scrimped and saved for. they prefer someone like susi. someone like susi on the other hand does not prefer them, which they do not know. they think susi is somewhat inferior, because she is a woman and stands below heinz. as a woman susi is lower, as a person, who occupies a rank in society, she is on the other hand somewhat higher than heinz.

that's too complicated for someone, who always had nothing but road signs in front of him, almost all his life.

that's completely incomprehensible to someone, who always only had dishes and heinz in front of her, almost all her life.

this scene takes place, because the father has to take early retirement, a place is already reserved for him at the masked ball of pain, at the carnival ball, and because therefore the highest level of parental savings has been passed. daddy no longer stands with both feet firmly planted in the middle of life as before. he's standing in the shit up to his neck. that's very shaky ground.

life goes on it is true, but it passes heinz's parents by.

now all hopes are pinned on heinz, who will disappoint them.

what they have piled up and produced, belongs to heinz, they didn't make it after all. the important things for heinz now are his journeyman's exam, master craftman's exam, electrical shop.

the path of the savings is now: into heinz, stop at brigitte!

the latter is conducting dialogues with her womb in her mother's living room. brigitte is asking, whether the little unborn child is inside yet.

no, says brigitte's uterus, still empty. i'm sorry. but perhaps it'll work out next month.

so brigitte keeps her chin up. and she's still got the job at any rate, it belongs to her alone. never ever lonely!

the corpse of brigitte's mother lies on the settee and reads the newspaper gossip about the royals. in her home she is queen. brigitte unfortunately is not yet in her own home.

up there with nature

meanwhile up in the little farmhouse the interests of the labouring rural population are in conflict. the interests of people, who have never aroused the interest of anyone else at all, who themselves don't know, that they could have anything like an interest. nevertheless they believe themselves to be the petrol in the machine, and paula to be the sand in it.

asthma squeaks through the nose like a mouse that's been stepped on. asthma doesn't need to speak, to keep several people constantly in motion, in motion around him. paula's puny stomach, which will soon be fat and swollen, so that for the same money one could suddenly have many more pounds of paula, is up for auction. but nobody wants it. with a pig that would be an enormous gain in value. with paula it's a sign, that she was easy to get, too easy, and now it's all the harder to dispose of her.

nobody wants paula's stomach content alone, to bring up and love. nobody wants paula as person, with or without stomach appendage. there is not even a taker for paula's outer skin. after all one can't make any settee cushions or any patchwork rug out of it.

no one's mentioning paula's head. whoever takes paula's body and her labour power, gets paula's head thrown in. as a free gift or extra. the far-sighted people, who are discussing their property, their productive asset called erich, might regard paula's head as a bad thing, which thinks too much and for that reason can no longer be properly guided.

asthma breathes laboriously through his gills and groans for his dinner. a retired official can make demands. paula who wants erich, can also make demands, but not get anything. erich's mother hurls herself towards the hot stove, where everything is simmering and bubbling. hardly has dada, who is already having difficulty speaking, croaked out his orders, than the goulash is in front of him.

result: paula's not coming into this house, except over the bodies of three grown persons. there's no more work needing to be done, we do our work ourselves, the women do the women's work, the man erich does the men's work, which is considerable. in addition erich is also important for bringing in money. money is almost more important and harder to get than work. we're never short of work, but often of money.

mr bandleader asthma is in charge. he conducts this orchestra of cripples without speaking. momma's hip complaint adds spice to it all, ensuring that things never get boring in kitchen, cellar, stall and bed. it really makes the work varied and go with a swing.

as a former official asthma has been trained to give orders. but asthma has a talent for it. asthma can't breathe any more, but his carefully trained gifts still get put to full use. a thorough federal railways training, it lasts a lifetime, longer even than the federal railways themselves. paula has no say and no business here.

paula sits around in her sunday dress. her slapped head lies hidden in her kicked stomach. she has rolled up into a ball like a hedgehog. without spines. her hands, which have not yet had to cope with a dressmaking examination, hold the whole frail fabric together. dressmaking provides no garland. the two of them don't know each other well enough yet, paula and dressmaking. in paula's head there appears a little bud, might dressmaking not after all have been better than erich. the bud is immediately torn out and trampled underfoot. in paula's heart the last stalk of love wilts silently away. in the sink the dishes doze sleepily away in their familiar surroundings. a new load of blows is gathering in the rancid fat of the family frying pan, if paula doesn't get to work on them right away. erich got to work on paula, that didn't get either of them anywhere, except land paula further in the shit, which she was already up to her neck in anyway. basically it's even set erich back in his career as driver and moped rider. a child can eat one out of house and home if it wants to.

hopefully the moped will win in this conflict of interests, hopes erich. so after erich has announced this decision, for the moped, against paula, into asthma's frog eyes, he mounts the victorious moped and races westwards into the setting sun. asthma is relieved. he'll knock the moped, this useless waste of money, out of the lad yet, one thing at a time.

paula's furious parents tear down the mountain, into paula's arms, a few more times into paula and out again in and out of paula, who has not even washed the dishes, all that's left of her is a couple of bones and feathers.

the west, however, is filled with erich. in the west new summer visitors, female ones too, have arrived.

now erich's skills at love at last come into their own.

paula suffers so much, she almost goes mad. she thinks, that her mind is running away out of every orifice, out of every orifice a little bit of mind, until it's empty. she runs her poor head against the wall again and again, her good parents are happy, that they can save themselves the bother of more thrashings, paula's taking care of it herself, well done.

there is no female solidarity to be expected from her mother. if she has to croak because of cancer, then paula can at least suffer a little in her head, which is much less serious than the physical pain, which mummy will shortly be facing. her father says now you can go on with the dressmaking, so that you can support your child.

paula squeaks pitifully no, she wants to be with her child, once it has arrived, then she wants to be there to meet her child from the train, and be around it all the time. she doesn't want to be a working momma, which a child suffers from. paula would rather suffer herself.

her dada is of course sorry now, that he never beat paula to death that time over the dressmaking, but now it's too late.

paula lies in wait for erich. she is no longer doing it for herself personally, she's doing it for the coming baby's life, that's due to come, and which is more important than she is.

she's almost indifferent to erich now, but to the child, if it could speak, erich would not be a matter of indifference, but dada. paula lies in wait behind the hazel bush, behind the elder bush or the birch wood bench.

with a war cry she jumps out at poor erich, who is coming from work so tired and weary. he is tired tired tired tired tired. his hands are hardly human any more, but more tree-like, like roots. erich slavers towards his home port and the evening. paula taxes erich's last reserves. and yet she has no interest in the man erich anymore, only in erich as future dad. she flings herself forward, clings to his back and talks about love and the child. paula tells of her feelings, which exist for erich. paula feels nothing at all for erich any more, erich even less than nothing for paula. but paula left school so recently, that she doesn't yet know the many words, with which one can say feelings. erich was never in school long enough, for him to know the words for something spiritual.

except for beer and schnapps. haha. schnapps, beer or wine is always brought up as a joke here at the mention of something spiritual.

a good joke.

paula says i need you erich and our child needs you too, perhaps even more than i need you, erich, even though i need you so much!

because so many people need him, erich slowly grows angry. since he is too clumsy, to ward these people off, he hits out like a madman, but often only hits himself. recently he often hits paula, which provides him with a certain satisfaction.

erich grasps, that all of a sudden his decisions and actions have become important for another person. that someone is DEPENDENT on him. that someone is at his MERCY in a way. that produces a nice new feeling. erich wants to test the new feeling as to its usefulness.

niki lauda has tested a lot too, even fantastic formula I cars.

that shoots through erich's head.

the two of them go into the old barn, it doesn't matter now anyway. paula has already endured so much, this is a proper holiday by comparison. at last she can lie quietly on her back and rest.

a flock of birds flies over the mown field into the forest, one behind the other, autumn will soon be here.

you can't expect descriptions of nature here for your money as well! this isn't the cinema after all.

paula lies very quietly and peacefully on her back. she has a section of the hard-worked back of erich, who is fumbling about with her there, in sight, but she can rest a little too and look up at the blue sky, it's already getting cold, soon the first snow clouds will appear. only a future refuses to appear. a mist is rising from the ground, the forest turns into a wall, the pale trunks disappear in the darkness. nature is pitiless, thinks paula. it is more than a match for a human being, it is an elemental force.

is that not a little deer over there? the evening news will soon begin on television!

at last paula can rest a little and perhaps still bind erich to her.

one can forget the slight pain of it, there are worse pains, which paula could name. love is a lesser pain in the hierarchy of pain. then, as erich rises from her stomach unbound, unimpressed, wipes himself and stows it away again, buttons himself up, a hope falls away from paula again down into the rotting straw. but if one has lost a hope, one has at least been able to rest. lying down is good for the baby too.

there is not the least tenderness in paula. there is nothing at all in paula. when all hopes have at last fallen from paula, she will be as light as a feather, like a kitten or a chick.

all the butchers! pork butchers! joiners, watch-

makers, bakers and chimney sweeps have disappeared over the horizon. behind the crows.
dressmaking is just packing its cases, it wants to catch the last postbus.
love hasn't even unpacked and put away its things.
work has become a case for treatment, it smoothes out the sheets in the hospital bed.
there is not the least love in paula.
if there is something in paula, then it's hate, which grows and grows.
these feelings didn't enter her of their own accord, some people had to work hard at it.
darkness falls, some animals begin to rustle in the forest, something stirs in the fox's den, two tired men quickly cross the village street, they want to get home, to their family and to the tv. lights come on. in some kitchens some children are shouting. mother puts the evening meal on the table. a headlamp pushes slowly through the fog. no one thinks of the forest as a landscape. the forest is a place of work. this is not a country story after all!
there is not the least hope in paula any more.

at this point we have to interrupt brigitte's fate a little abruptly

since we hold brigitte's fate in our hands, we can interrupt it at any point we like.
brigitte's feelings do no undergo any change, they remain always constant for heinz, and heinz rebuffs them again and again.
here we're going to talk about feelings, but not about facts.

brigitte is incapable of feeling. consequently there is nothing to be said about brigitte.

brigitte makes no facts, the facts burst upon her.

now brigitte is making a pullover for heinz.

the pullover only progresses slowly, because brigitte has to devote her working time to work and her free time to the surveillance, servicing and sexual welfare of heinz.

allegedly every woman, who puts on a bra sewn by brigitte, will feel like a queen.

brigitte will only feel like a queen in her beautiful home.

in addition brigitte has the capacity to bear children, which not everyone has. she hopes to be allowed to bear such a child soon.

since brigitte has known heinz, she feels an urge, to bear a child. if that's not a feeling, what on earth is a feeling?

brigitte's heart has spoken, it said heinz. brigitte follows this heart wherever it leads, that is to heinz.

there she gets a kick in the backside a hundred times, but the 101st time brigitte can announce the good news, that the child is to be expected. then the sun will shine for brigitte too. brigitte is going to buy herself a bikini already for this sunny day.

the child will be a wanted child. the child is wanted by brigitte, but not by heinz.

admittedly that's inconvenient, but to make up the child's start in life will be made very much easier by ownership of an electrical goods shop.

brigitte herself had a difficult start in life.

often brigitte feels that something is her own fault, which is actually someone's else's fault.

she thinks for example, that it's her own fault, if she

has to work on the line. when it's solely heinz's fault, who doesn't want to marry her and rescue her from the line.

brigitte has often seen in the cinema, that it is difficult, if one has to live with a feeling of guilt.

with no events worth mentioning brigitte's curriculum vitae will grow less and less. in future we can limit ourselves to providing a few notes on the general situation, in which we always briefly mention brigitte's particularly disagreeable situation.

everything, which is still to come now, consists of a waiting and an eavesdropping on oneself, to ascertain whether movement and quickening is at last taking place there.

the situation is clarified and explained.

no more events will take place until the one big event.

work continues to take place.

that is painful enough.

birth too is a painful experience, which must be endured however, so that the presentation of the child can take place.

after all the birth of the child does not take place to please the child, but to please the man who gets the present. heinz's family name and all the excellent security that provides are presents enough for the child.

child and wife are for ever in heinz's debt.

one can already guarantee the child, that in future it will not get much pleasure in life, except when the parents-in-law or important customers are visiting.

the mother's humiliation will certainly be taken out on the children, the first will be beaten and damaged, then the next will right away be produced. a child can become a victim of general wear and tear or of big city traffic, one must be kept in reserve. it's best to have one child in stock to take account of wear and tear.

and perhaps the child is better than the sewing machine. one can go for a walk in the fresh air with the child, not with the machine. the machine has no heart, the child has.

apart from that the machine is in the factory and the child at home in well-ordered surroundings.

it can take many months, here it's many pages, before the child pops its head out of the womb like a worm out of the apple, perhaps we won't even get that far here. perhaps we'll have to break off before then. but that doesn't matter, we know what's going to happen. life goes on without surprises, but within proper channels.

today brigitte enters the desolate home of her desolate mother just as hopelessly as ever, and there's heinz already standing in the toilet too, giving himself a hand job to start with, so that later he won't be so greedy and can take better care, that not a milligram too much comes out at the wrong time and in the wrong hole, so that's he's not caught and has to develop into a trapped instead of an independent entrepreneur.

squealing with passion, as she later explains to heinz, brigitte hails blows down on him. next brigitte lies herself down and heinz on top, in their conservative way. she has a bag of almond croissants by her which she immediately hurls aside, to keep her hands free, to be able to hold heinz tight, so as not to have to let go, to be nicely stuffed.

meanwhile the almond croissants roll away across the dirty floorboards. throughout the intensive fucking

with heinz, brigitte thinks about the almond croissants, which are now dirty and ruined, pity. heinz
briefly thinks, will it look as dirty in my house too,
if I perhaps have to go through with the wedding
after all?
brigitte who has guessed his thoughts, replies no,
when its my own, then i'll work to look after it and
maintain it.
only for my own.
heinz also is only interested in his own. on that the
two of them agree.
only one's own is really one's own. what one's got,
one's got, what one hasn't got, one must try to get.
if one doesn't get, then it's of no interest.
other people's property is taboo. heinz is brigitte's
property, therefore taboo. taboo for susi and all the
rest of you.
heinz quickly wants to withdraw, before it's too late
and in brigitte's interior, but brigitte snaps shut, her
thoughts admittedly are still with the almond croissants and the crushed new handbag on the floor, but
her physical powers are automatically and entirely
concentrated on heinz.
heinz feels pleasure and cries out loud.
brigitte would most of all like to stuff all the muck
under the sofa into his trap, until it flows out of his
ears again.
heinz cries out loud yet again, so that one notices
he's having fun with his handle and the handling.
brigitte emits forced grunts. her eyeballs follow the
path of the almond croissants right into the middle
of the dirt on the floor. momma's an old cow, for
not sweeping up, when she doesn't even have to look
after a man.

heinz cries out ever more quickly, at ever shorter intervals. he enjoys it so much, the pig.

brigitte would like to slam his roaring head against the wall. can't he at least do it quietly? the kid'll squirt out of him anyway, whether he's quiet now or noisy.

mummy is meanwhile sitting discreetly and cleared away in the kitchen. she is completely silent, so as not to threaten the happiness of her child in there with an ill-considered remark.

in the living room brigitte's happiness is still taking place.

heinz shoots his load with a bloodcurdling cry. the neighbours will complain. but faced by the young businessman they will retire, tail between their legs. apologetically.

the bloodcurdling cry proves, that only love moves the world. that love and heinz both together move the world. in person.

brigitte is unmoved, but she is full of slime, full of evil-smelling slime. therefore brigitte does not move the world, but love moves the world.

brigitte almost has to vomit, it hasn't been as bad for a long time. heinz hurries to his mates on the sports field. brigitte wipes the poor almond croissants, she feels so sorry for them.

now paula

now paula is slowly getting fatter, which looks very ugly. feelings of shame rise in paula. after a long time feelings again, but not good ones.

often, when paula, protected by a waterproof cape,

but otherwise unprotected, goes to do the shopping in the village, little stones strike the back of her head, her arse, her stomach, her calves or the shopping bag, worst of all the shopping bag and in it the bottle to return, which gets broken.

first of all something in paula broke, now the returnable bottle is broken as well.

paula has the feeling, that the whole village has made use of this unfavourable moment in time, to display their children and their legitimate worries with men.

a whole lot of money and goods is standing around everywhere on the street.

paula has no money and has not been good.

paula is regarded as a future mother, but not as a future housewife.

paula is as good as dead.

the other women are as good as alive, which is not yet alive however. their husbands always act very lively.

if once one of them dies of cirrhosis of the liver instead of cancer, then that makes a change. one can exchange exotic symptoms. sometimes a bloody forestry worker is taken by jeep to the hospital during shopping hours.

as if from one mouth a frightful cry rings out from the legitimately pregnant women. they press their hands against their all-too-sensitive bellies and hobble home to their mothers and female relatives. there they bury their heads in diverse laps and fear for their unborn brats, who after this sight could come into the world as cripples.

in the diverse households the legitimately pregnant are put to bed, reminded of the expected infants, and then tucked up warm.

words of comfort ring out, which mostly assert, it could have happened to one's own man, but that thank god it's happened to another man, whose little woman must now cry her eyes out. soon the tears dry up again, the quivering stomachs slowly calm down, from noses comes a comforted sniffing.

paula, who calls no such man her own, makes herself very tiny and scuttles under the shadow of a roof. she melts away into nothing in her surroundings.

while her female colleagues bury their heads in their pillows and enjoy the heaviness of their full bodies, paula has become one with the darkness.

diverse grandmothers in diverse households do the heavy housework for their daughters, who are enjoying their off season at the moment. paula enjoys nothing, least of all an off season.

since paula enjoyed a forbidden pleasure long ago, she is not to be allowed to enjoy anything at all any more.

while everyone watches the process of sowing wild oats and locking horns by the young men and greets especially large knocked off horns with applause, paula walks silently home from the shadows. as she does so a horn often strikes paula a serious blow.

and the faces of the old men, who can no longer raise an arm or a leg from their fireside seats, take on an almost otherworldly glow, and they're pleased when paula is struck by a horn.

they're thinking about their own time of sowing wild oats and locking horns.

that time is long gone, which is a tragedy.

the wild oat sowers crowd together on the benches along the main road, the principal traffic artery, and in front of the co-op shop. sometimes an especially brave sower collides with an especially rare make of car. howls ring out. sometimes even a bloody head lies beside the horn with which he got stuck in so lustily just a little while ago. sometimes even a bloody body lies beside head and horns. then the forest has to look for a new man again. so much sap and power in a crowd, every heart beats faster than before. hurrah.

once again paula practises being invisible.

but once again she's at the centre of things, where it's louder and jollier than anywhere else. paula, our heroine.

although paula constantly tries to crawl into the ground, she is dug up again. and the young men always walk right behind paula for the purpose of sowing wild oats. they want to sow their wild oats and plough paula at the same time, because it's safe now.

they certainly won't have to pay for the child, but have some first class post-conception fun.

erich can also be spotted right at the middle of the pack, which hurts paula. erich always goes along, where everyone else is going, what many people think, that'll be the right thing to think and even more the right thing to do, thinks erich rightly. his hand, which was made and trained for coarser things, clutches the handlebar of his moped, the moped is his best friend in good times and in bad. the other hand clutches the beer bottle, which will soon make him forget the good times and the bad.

paula cannot change any of this behaviour.

she tries to get close to erich. she can only find erich in the pack: immediately all the wild oat sowers surround her.

paula demands a decision from erich regarding herself.

when asthma is miles away, up the mountain, and momma is there too where she belongs, that is at asthma's side under asthma's thumb on the mountain, where she is making him a hot foot bath and dunking his ugly toes with their poor circulation into the hot water, then erich is suddenly supposed to come to a decision concerning paula. erich looks into his beer, and the beer looks out of its bottle with its death's head, which is supposed to be a reminder, that under certain circumstances alcohol can kill, if work and the circumstances of life don't kill one first, so when erich looks into his beer, then he suddenly feels as if he could really come to a decision.

ultimately however erich doesn't come to his own decision, but asthma's decision.

erich comes to the decision: no.

erich certainly feels sorry for paula. he has no memory of the activity which he performed in order to cause paula's condition. he cannot say, whether it was nice or not. erich can experience nothing as beautiful except his machines, which he runs into the ground one after the other.

sex only does his cock good, it doesn't reach the brain, which speed does reach, which does his whole body good.

when one races along at full speed, then everything bad seems to fall away, first of all work, which is the worst thing which can happen to one. but it has to be done. paula is bad too, but she doesn't have to be married.

paula is one of the bad things, which fall away from

one, when one races along the country road at top speed.

at last paula is finally allowed to go home. even from a distance one recognises a woman who is returning home with an intense, expectant gaze, a maternal smile, a careful step and a tugging in her innards.

it's our paula.

paula grins like a death's head, but one which is only 15 years old. welcome home, paula. as every other day the aborting housework is already waiting.

her momma hopes that the little grandchild will after all flush out of paula still unformed and incapable of living, if she only gets down on her knees properly, if she lifts heavy buckets with hot dirty soapy water, if she only slogs away enough, little paula. but nothing slips and slides, except the sweat, which streams from every pore. there must be a lock and key in front of it down there, suspects her momma.

the thought of feeding and dressing the baby with the earlier dressmaking is pushed far away by paula. it doesn't count. erich, the breadwinner. that's what paula learned from her momma. and from her dada too, who admittedly almost beat her to death, but always regularly fed her. paula's dada has always done his duty by his family, which erich must do too.

when paula's thoughts wander especially far, then they wander to the forces of nature, about which paula knows, that they are stronger than any human being. just as one cannot fight against nature, so one cannot fight against a natural law of this nature, paula still remembers from school. the natural law in this case is called erich, who however has never heard the word law.

so paula also realises, how small she is compared to

the law of nature. a grain of dust. a grain of dust in the desert.

what can a human being do against the elemental force of the force of nature, nothing. a documentary film on television yesterday said that, says paula often too.

brigitte's further fate

brigitte's further fate is actually concluded and need not be mentioned here again. the reason we neverthe-less mention it, is, that it's simple to describe, because it's concentrated on a single point: heinz, from which it is true there can be wrong turnings and little deviations, but to whom one can always find the right path. brigitte's fate is finished here, it only has to be carried out.

today is again one of those days, on which brigitte approaches her goal with particular determination, by getting up, because she has to go to the factory. the factory is the little deviation, the goal is the eve-ning with heinz. brigitte slips into her dress, which is a skirt and a pullover, and emphasises her female form, which is indeed its purpose.

the factory is the waiting room, the workplace is heinz.

paula on the other hand.

paula also has other interests, which she will be able to realise with erich's help. paula's interests are going to the cinema, holidays in italy, television at home and bringing up children at home and outside. paula doesn't only want to get erich, but build some-thing with him: a household. a little kingdom in common in which one can do as one likes, which is what a household should be. paula has a love for erich, which has grown smaller but is nevertheless still present, because she has heard, that one must come to love one person alone, because this man is the dada of her children, but whom one must also love as a man, which will take over from and replace the love of one's beloved parents.

paula doesn't love her parents at all.

nevertheless paula sees a future full of love before her.

paula produces love out of herself like a hormone.

brigitte on the other hand.

brigitte needs heinz, and brigitte needs heinz's future shop, and she needs her parents-in-law out of the way, then she needs work, work and more work, to make the shop prettier and bigger.

what brigitte has at the moment: work work and more work. if one invests one's energy in something of one's own, then it returns to one several times over, then one can easily get by without love and its outgrowths and varieties.

so brigitte wants to fundamentally improve her situation.

paula wants to fundamentally improve her situation and find happiness at the same time as well.

brigitte doesn't care about happiness in itself, i.e. she thinks that affluence heinz and happiness are one and the same. that's why heinz is quite enough for her, brigitte is modest.

paula is immodest, she wants the same thing as brigitte, but she wants a beautiful radiant halo around it. she wants to show people all the time, how much one loves the child, the husband, the house, the washing machine, the refrigerator and the garden. ALL of it.

love can move mountains, but not erich. love can move mountains, but not change erich into a loving human being. erich is unpractised at being loved, he has never experienced it himself.

apart from that love cannot produce a refrigerator. if there is no refrigerator etc., then one only has husband and children to love, those are too few objects for paula's great great love. there is sooo much love in paula, which is lying idle and craving worthwhile objects.

brigitte only wants to own and as much as possible. brigitte simply wants to HAVE and to HOLD ON to it.

paula wants to have and to love, and to show people, that one has, and what one has and loves.

even if paula didn't love erich any more, she would still have to show people, that she loves erich. that's a lot of effort at simulation, but it must be done. even if one cannot love erich any more, there are still lots of things, which erich has bought with his money, which one can love as substitute.

brigitte wants to have and multiply as much as possible. that's a simple goal, any child can understand that.

and the astonished world around, which is used to all of it since time immemorial, stands by and watches, applauds and places bets, who'll be the winner and who'll come second. sometimes there's also a loser.

today brigitte is once again not yet pregnant.

only a pregnancy could produce a change in brigitte's life and in this plot.

today brigitte is once again, as so often, terribly afraid, that susi, the girls' grammar school pupil,

could get pregnant before her, for which unfortunately the most basic conditions are lacking.

because susi is not yet a woman, but still a girl.

susi is still saving. susi can still pack her sports bag
to play tennis with easy cheerfulness, nothing dirty
has entered her life yet.

heinz doesn't think he's something dirty, but a clean
young lad, his skittle playing too is clean.

the uncleanest thing in heinz's life is certainly brigitte, the black spot on his white shirt.

the young businessman unmistakably directs his
ambition towards susi.

brigitte wants to direct heinz's ambition unmistakably towards her.

brigitte forgets, that one doesn't need any ambition,
to get her. heinz only needs to leave the house, and
he stumbles over brigitte.

one day even susi's mother notices, that there is a
dark shadow, our heinz, behind susi. her mother
notices with her mother's instinct, that this shadow
is dark with uncleanliness.

she asks, whether she should intervene. but susi only
laughs sweetly and says no. i can manage it myself.

later her mother says to father, that hopefully susi
will retain her innocence and cheerfulness for a long
time to come.

while heinz crawls after susi and casts a shadow on
her tennis dress, brigitte is afraid, that she won't
get pregnant. but brigitte will certainly get pregnant,
because her body is reliable, even if brigitte's head
flips out. this fear will continue for a while yet. no
further reports. end of fate for brigitte.

from paula's life there are only a few more episodes
to report, which have such a gigantic superstructure,

that it in no way corresponds to the significance of these stories. desires, dreams and illusions congeal into an indigestible mass in paula's head. it's amusing to watch as paula constantly falls flat on her face. it's amusing for those standing upright to watch, as paula constantly falls flat on her face in accordance with the laws of gravity and of love.

when brigitte turns her attention to the millionaire villas in her magazines, then she immediately calculates the dimensions of her future family house in her head, then right away thinks about where the office premises should go and where we'll break through a door.

when paula reads the same thing, then she's right in the middle of it, then the house is already there, appearing out of thin air, then the huge garden is already there and set down in a clean environment, like a stage set, and happy young people romp about in it: erich with his young family and the two german shepherd dogs as well.

it's an all-encompassing romp. and the people from the village stand at the fence and gape in envy.

paula often thinks about the feeling of being envied and admired, brigitte often thinks about the feeling of having, acquiring and owning.

paula thinks about the effect, without being able to create the conditions for it. erich will not be able to manage either, which paula cannot know yet.

brigitte takes care of the cause, brigitte sticks with the businessman heinz, then the effect will appear automatically.

brigitte – the town child.

paula – the country child.

after that paula and brigitte think in unison about their wedding. that takes up some time.
with brigitte it takes up all her working time and almost all her free time.
with paula it takes up all her time, which is working time.

the hours trickle away

the hours take their inevitable course, and paula will soon be ready to deliver, if things go on like this. the midwife is already waiting.
paula's pointless efforts, which all concentrate on erich, go further than one has ever seen anyone go here.
when evening comes, then people take their places in the best seats in the house. they take the whole family. from there they observe in person or through binoculars paula's idiotic efforts.
the village community is identical with the general public.
the general public definitely approves of paula's absurd and humiliating efforts, to catch a valuable trophy.
the valuable head of game is called erich.
paula must legalise her disagreeable condition.
for that she needs erich. in order to bash down precious timber for building and other uses, the valuable head of game erich, needs only himself: erich.
paula has made a mess, now she has to swallow it too. all by herself. erich, the red deer, must help her swallow the mess down, so that the plate is emptied more quickly.

erich sits upon his throne, which is situated in the middle of the inn.

paula enters and displays her little tricks, her knowledge and skills, which are all minimal.

it's just like the circus, only much funnier.

unfortunately erich doesn't catch much of it, because he has long ago fallen into a drunken stupor, as paula takes the run-up for a double back somersault with twist.

no tap on the shoulder, slap on the back, poke in the ribs, no salutation however coarse fetches erich back from the land of dreams into the harsh reality of paula's presence.

until now no one has really taken erich as being all there. now he's given paula a fat stomach, and suddenly he's accepted as all there. previously everyone just thought erich too dopey, too stupid, to have the skirts off the summer visitors, too weak in the head, to get his driving licence even at the third attempt, too feeble-minded and weak to hit the tree trunk with the axe. everyone thought he would hit his own noddle instead of the tree. but he only cut and shook paula to the quick. until now everyone saw erich only as a workhorse, unlike themselves, who are all workhorses too, but don't feel that they are. now everyone pays erich their respects with regard to cracking paula.

paula has been cracked no doubt about it.

then erich's shoulder joints squeak agonisingly on their hinges, then the fist familiar with the axe must grip for the unfamiliar act of shaking hands. congratulations erich.

then the free beers, free glasses of schnapps and wine, the free hair ruffling and free of charge rib pokes, and the jocular kicks up the arse for nothing really pile up.

yet again one such sneaky but well-meant kick lifts erich off his hinges, with a crash.

then erich falls back into his regular seat like a lifeless bag of muscles.

erich has never had so much experience of success before.

unfortunately erich – just like paula – can no longer remember the occasion, which has brought him the title grand impregnator, not with all the will in the world, after all no hurtling moped ride took him there, only a quiet woodland path.

everything has been wiped away in erich.

nevertheless it's fun now to appear among the men and lads as a person to be respected. erich has never had fun, now he has a lot of fun all at once. little man, very big.

at ten o'clock in the evening entrance of the very pregnant paula, entry of the bar by the future illegitimate mother.

shouting, stamping of feet, whistles, applause. now there'll be fun.

the last bets are placed.

paula no longer has a grade, such as even eating apples must have. paula has no market value any more.

paula bears the consequences for what she has done before her. paula wants to recite her poem. it goes in free verse something like this, that erich must come home, because it's already late and erich must be up for his hard work tomorrow, that paula will soon open up to let out a child, that paula and her unborn child are waiting for erich. no matter how long it takes. in other words: your wife plus child inside are waiting for you, erich. and please please, give me your name erich.

but erich cannot even say his name any more. once again paula has come too late.

everyone thinks, that erich, if he must give way, should only give way, once the child is already present, and paula's reduction in value has become a complete devaluation.

when someone is devalued so much, then they are all thereby enhanced in value. paula's humiliation compensates them for their own, sometimes much more terrible humiliations.

suddenly they have all become persons again in comparison with a non-person.

we are gathered here today in this place, to assess and to value paula's attempts to drag erich home to her. the judges hold up their marks.

paula pounces on erich and desperately tries to get the drunk, now also puking, person home. paula tugs at erich's protruding parts. sometimes the protruding parts of erich snap back like rubber bands, sometimes they also strike paula with full force. all around eyes and flies almost burst with enjoyment.

paula believes, she has a right to erich.

the air is thick with smoke, beer fumes, sweat and dirty jokes.

paula, the pregnant almost 16-year-old girl, tightens her muscles like a farmhorse and heaves the drunk man to his feet, but she doesn't get far with her sweet burden.

the hands of erich's forest colleagues tear the precious catch from her hands again. with combined strength.

paula's solitary strength is powerless against the combined strength of the lords of the forest. paula has lost and has to let go of erich. even so paula was lucky, that no one kicked her in the stomach and damaged something there.

paula's mother would have been very well disposed to any damage to the child in paula's stomach. it would be best, if a premature birth or a miscarriage could take place.

unfortunately after all these months the child is probably already capable of life outside paula.

so erich is propped up on the bar room bench again, he has hardly been aware of anything that's been going on. weighed down by the child, paula creeps homewards. paula would rather be weighed down by erich and have lost the child. several times paula falls flat on her face, because it's so dark. all these deadly tricks still don't kill the kid in her stomach.

sobbing and bawling it's home to bed, paula has pushed the child in her stomach in front of her the whole way, to where she's at home. like a snuffling hunting dog, nose to the ground, paula reaches the hearth at home, that is far from homely for paula.

paula folds her arms, which will soon hold her child, beneath her face, which will soon look down on her child, and hopes, that at least it'll be a boy and not a girl.

hopefully it will be a boy and not a girl, hopes paula.

the next day, already early in the morning, a beginning is made, to making paula scared of the labour pains, which are said to be very painful.

if paula had a man, then one would comfort, pamper and calm her before the labour pains.

and one day, when the air is particularly mild, paula is taken to hospital and squeezes the child out of herself and into the light of day with painstaking effort. while still in the ambulance paula decides, that the son will receive the name of the father, erich, but the daughter will receive the city name susanne. it's a girl. the daughter susanne has arrived.

erich is even less likely to marry you because of a girl than because of a lad, the disappointed parents threaten the hospital bed.

but paula's mother does like her, because she's such a sweet little thing. that is also what is expected on all sides from paula's mother.

susanne has become an illegitimate daughter.

paula has become an unmarried mother.

they are both female.

that is at once a stroke of luck, but also an obligation to behave like a human being and not like a female animal.

it is a fine obligation. much finer than erich's obligation to cut wood.

paula is only 16 years older than her daughter, nevertheless she is already close to giving up.

you have behaved no differently from an animal in the forest, because any of them can have a litter, but none of them can get married, an aunt, who has hurried to paula's bed from the city, where she's married, also earnestly admonishes. paula lies in the hospital bed, listens to the admonishments and bawls.

it's easy for the town aunt to be generous, because she married a baker from the city and she and the baker have a car.

so the town aunt generously promises, that she will

talk to erich and soften him up, which one has to do with men, if they don't do anything of their own accord.

apart from that men can sometimes easily be good-natured.

a constant drip will wear down a stone, wear down erich too presumably!

humiliate oneself and then wear him down: only way.

the town aunt also thinks, that it has turned out a sweet little thing. one must not make the child suffer.

and apart from that it is such a sweet clumsy little thing, even though paula's such an ugly fishbone.

first of all work has worn erich down, now the town aunt will soften him up.

we shall report later, what shape erich took after the softening up.

interim report

the glimmer of happiness, which means wife and mother for brigitte, is still absent today too.

today a walk in the park for demonstration purposes (new coat!) is taking place. on this walk there is a chance meeting with susi, who looks as if made entirely of gold and is taking the little son of her sister in a pram and a giant purebred shepherd dog with pedigree on a lead for a walk.

it is a picture planned with the greatest refinement. here nature has taken its optimum form, the fine purebred animal and susi, who is like that too, only a different species. in the light which falls through the foliage onto her head, susi looks like the incarnation of all mothers, who have ever been mothers. brigitte however thinks, that susi could never be a good mother, because she's an egotist and could never subordinate her interests to a child.

brigitte's misunderstanding is, that susi could very well subordinate her interests to a little child, if this child only squirts out of the right cock.

heinz's cock would be the wrong one. he can hardly manage to force feeling even from coarse brigitte.

how then from fine grained susi!

susi doesn't have a new coat like brigitte, but her casual-sporty walking outfit of expensive materials makes a much more perfect impression than brigitte's new spring coat. susi looks like this: mother and child out for a walk.

the beautiful dog completes the picture, its strength appears strangely subdued and gentle next to the pram and with susi.

let me be the wild man, whom you put on the chain and tame, susi, thinks heinz lustfully and with a trace of uncleanliness in his thoughts.

it is immediately apparent to everyone, how much susi loves the little child.

a picture without words.

pure and beautiful, as it should be.

brigitte right away feels vulgar and superficial in her new coat of wool and synthetic fibre. yet you liked it so much in the shop, fickle brigitte.

heinz immediately speaks to susi, the little thing looks right with you.

despite susi's emphatically maternal aura, heinz would more than anything like to get his cock into the starting position on the spot.

heinz somewhat prematurely has the feeling of a formula I driver before the start.

once again brigitte feels hate. the master craftsman's diploma, the future business, the savings of the parents-in-law, all of that seems to move out of reach again, heinz seems to concentrate entirely on susi with that skier's starting feeling, that he never has with brigitte.

susi already suits pretend motherhood so well, just imagine how well the real thing will suit her.

susi comes from quite different circles, heinz is just the man to brush such refined circles aside.

if anyone is right for this awkward task, then heinz.

susi too is in a much less combative mood today than usual.

no local folk costume groups, against whose dissolution one can be up in arms, no discussion groups, in which one can express one's opinion, no demonstration, which one can join.

susi explains, that this little baby in its pram doesn't know about all that yet, and that she proposes, to keep everything ugly away from it.

brigitte is up to her neck in ugliness.

shit isn't very nice.

susi gives brigitte tips about housekeeping, but also tips about bringing up children, she uses various psychological foreign words, which brigitte does not understand.

nevertheless brigitte would certainly be a better mother than susi, so she thinks. at the same time susi lets it drop, that she is still too young for children, but that the one and only, special man, will knock the nonsense out of her and one day choose her for motherhood despite her youth.

then susi will answer YES.

susi literally says: perhaps someone will knock this nonsense out of me.

brigitte doesn't understand very much of what susi is saying.

but brigitte does understand, that heinz sees himself in the role of this one and only and susi in the role of his property. however she, brigitte, is his property. thank god susi doesn't take up this offer, because she doesn't yet know, what that can possibly mean, a business of one's own.

susi simply does not know yet, what a real man is and what he looks like: like heinz.

heinz chivalrously takes the dog's lead: strength united with elegance.

so heinz creates a togetherness between himself and susi, which is impenetrable and indestructible for brigitte. forced to the edge of existence by these two figures of light, brigitte sees the following picture before her inadequately trained inner eyes: she cleans the shit out of the lavatory bowl once again today with heinz's hairs in it. she would then like to stick his whole head in it.

and yet today the date is so favourable and the clothes are so new. if it doesn't work out today, then never. today or never.

if brigitte can present him with a real son and heir, then susi and her nephew will pale into insignificance by comparison. then heinz will learn to distinguish the right child from the wrong child: his own flesh and blood from susi's nephew.

no sooner said than done.

heinz, i love you so much, says brigitte mechanically, having at last reached home. her hair shines reddish in the sun, that comes from the dye, which is in it. in heinz's balls there has for some time now been a desire, which must be satisfied today.

unbuttoning and into brigitte only takes a moment.

and today we can announce, that something has clicked at last between these two young people, though it will only become apparent in a couple of weeks.

and so in the end brigitte after all will come to have a fate.

at last some light from heinz also fell upon brigitte.

today heinz knocked brigitte up. congratulations.

and so brigitte will not after all have to end her life in cold and loneliness, which otherwise she would have had to do.

brigitte's rise is a result of painstaking attention to detail. brigitte could settle the battle of the sexes once more in her favour.

brigitte will then certainly also be a perfect worker in the shop and an attentive assistant.

brigitte's happiness is not due to chance, rather she had to fight hard for it.

brigitte believed, that there is another life apart from the life on the line, and brigitte was right: there is another life besides the life on the production line, there's heinz.

where there's a will, there's a way.

gitti has found this way. thank heavens she is naturally fertile and not infertile, otherwise the whole thing would have come to nothing in the end after all.

well done, brigitte's body. child-bearing capacity is the victor. in particular womb and ovaries.

perhaps susi has such organs too, but she has to provide the evidence first.

brigitte is on top now at any rate.

first foot forward to the work of child-bearing and to the work in the electrical goods shop, brigitte

do you have wombs too? let's hope so! as we see from brigitte's example, who did not let this important female organ go to waste on the line, but through heinz got it into full working order.

all's well that ends well.

asthma's death makes it possible

the conversation between town aunt and country aunt only bore fruit – as the sexual intercourse between erich and paula bore fruit – because asthma suddenly kicked the bucket.

all of a sudden asthma is lying in the dark cemetery earth, from where he cannot do anything to anyone any more.

erich's momma, however, feels the exact opposite around herself, that is, a sudden unbelievable emptiness, through which the orders of an ex-civil servant no longer resound.

momma lays her deformed bones down in an easy chair and only twitches from time to time like a hunting dog, as if an instruction, a request, which is an order, could sound from somewhere, but which will never sound again.

the dreadful wheezing, puffing and rattling are as if blown away. silence has fallen.

nothing sounds and resounds through the kitchen any more.

so from one day to the next, one ends up with an unfulfilled life, while asthma's mortal remains have just been laid to rest.

momma had thrown herself into the funeral preparations as if possessed, as if once again she wanted to devote all her energies to the only proper goal: asthma. then it was over and there was silence.

only old grandmomma is still alive, who long ago when she was not even fourteen sent her into service and to the first drawn cock of her life. momma is now well and truly repaying her.

that grandmomma had long ago and already at the age of 12 been sent into service and to the first drawn cock that came her way, that the country folk with their short memory had long forgotten. only grandmomma still knows, but no one listens to her any more.

anyhow it's still nicer, to bully one's momma, if one has no husband to wait on any more, than to do nothing at all. nasty words and death threats echo through the mountains.

paula's aunt bursts in as the old granny is in the middle of a crying fit, caused by the recently widowed asthmaless daughter. if you remember. she wants to detach erich from the family bonds and stick him to paula. she says, among other things, the poor little helpless child will have to grow up without a dada, is it not enough that your own children had to grow up most of the time without dadas? a child needs a dada just as much as it needs a momma. a child needs a firm hand just as much as the mother's gentle one a child needs both parents to be together not apart it is better for the child of course paula did something that was dirty and stupid but she's still very young, you were young once too and paula will behave herself in future and not do anything dirty again.

and erich isn't so innocent either, it always takes two, although the man's urge is stronger and so he can't be blamed so much.

but a man can get by alone, whereas a woman, paula, can't get by alone so easily with the child, and she needs erich's firm hand too, she needs a man's firm hand too.

and the child needs its dada: erich.

who knows, whether erich is the dada at all, retorts the angry woman darkly, if a girl goes with one man, then if she has to she'll go with several men. who knows, perhaps my erich isn't the dada at all, who knows.

the usual humiliation is followed by the usual silence.

now the blameless town aunt gets to feel some of paula's humiliation as well. for that paula will get a mighty box on the ears, she promises herself that.

but soon the wedding bells will ring!

but soon the wedding bells will ring! ding dong ding dong.

erich's momma pushes and pushes against every obstacle, but where once a thick concrete wall stood: asthma, this time everything gives way, is soft as butter, it's an annoying experience, which one can no longer properly cope with at this age. suddenly to be the object of pleas, suddenly to have to fulfil something, suddenly to stand above someone lower, who is pleading, that is terribly confusing for the otherwise so disciplined woman.

this woman too is sorely afflicted.

one man has already died off, who's left then? nobody at all.

momma says, it is hard, to have to give a person away. one has to be very strong, to bear something like that. momma is very strong, she hauls two heavy metal buckets fill of hot swill as if they were nothing at all, although she is nothing but skin and bone.

anyone who can endure asthma for even a fraction of the time, which momma endured him, is a strong person.

whom can she hate now, if everyone has left the house?

answer: there is only old granny left, whom one can hate, and who is now even a greatgranny.

so all the hate falls on greatgranny!

spotlights on.

in town talk the town aunt pleads, that momma should make two young people happy, in the magazine language, of which she has full command

say yes, give nature its due and let it run its natural course, everything else will sort itself out then anyway. that's what she says.

first nature took its inexorable course, now happiness is supposed to make an entry. the town aunt thinks, momma should not close her mind to this natural course of nature.

at last erich's confused momma opens her mind to the course of nature. she steps out of the way, so that nature can shoot in, and there's nature already! the wedding can take place.

there will be a beautiful white wedding.

perhaps erich will give up alcohol too, recommends the town aunt over-enthusiastically at which point she is definitely barking up the wrong tree.

so there will be a beautiful white wedding.

dully erich agrees, he couldn't care less.

either he hands over his money to dada, apart from what he drinks or mopeds away, or he hands over a little to paula and the bastard.

this is not a country story.

this is not a love story either, even if it looks like it.

although it is apparently about the country and about love, it is nevertheless not about the countryside and about love.

the subject of this novel is paula.

erich makes the decisions for the subject paula, and yet others make decisions about his physical strength, till his innards decompose towards an early death, in which alcohol does its bit. erich makes decisions about paula's life and the life of his daughter susanne.

for the time being the couple will live with paula's parents, who will let them have a room. they are happy to be getting a young couple and not paula and susanne alone.

and soon we shall be four, not just three! the young woman whispers one day. and soon we shall have an apartment of our own or a little house of our own, it won't be long.

and before long there will be savings, which we haven't got yet. at the moment we have only ourselves and our love.

and our happiness. we shall set to work happily and lovingly. then the result will be happy and loving too.

paula used up her happiness and her love long ago, or what she thought were happiness and love.

erich was never happy nor felt love anyway.

erich always only had his work, which he doesn't love and which doesn't make him happy.

both have susanne. and two hands, two hands each, which can knuckle down to it. the traces of the knuckling down hands will soon be found on susanne's body. until someone bigger and stronger will lay his hands on susanne, a bill or a tommy. certainly not the dear lord above.

who will himself personally bless and join these two young people, who have already blessed themselves with a little child. before that there is still catholic marriage instruction in the presbytery, where paula is treated like dirt. but one day too that will be forgotten.

one day the noose will tighten.

soon we shall describe a beautiful wedding, so that the plot doesn't get too disagreeable.

one must not describe only negative and ugly things.

the principal characters involved have a feeling of anticipation.

the principal characters involved are unfortunately almost incapable of feelings of anticipation by now.

you can't make a racehorse out of an old nag.

paula however has still retained her optimism.

paula is as grateful as a dog, it is terrible to have to watch paula's gratitude. her gratitude allows no room for joy.

paula is also relieved.

she is also in principle prepared for another birth.

the wedding preparations begin.

erich thinks the baby is sweet. but he is just a man and by nature doesn't see anything in small babies, explains paula, who is once again worthy of making explanations. paula is so happy she is so happy.

she smothers the little baby enthusiastically with kisses in front of everyone, as a momma should and must do.

erich loves his engines and his schnapps.

paula loves her husband and her child and her future house.

now everything will turn out for the best!

paula's kisses are even audible in the room next door.

now everything will turn out for the best.

about brigitte's womb

at last she begins to bloom and to thrive, and her still formless content blooms and thrives with her.

when the vomit rises for the first time early in the morning, she knows, that the day is no longer distant now. there can be no other reason, for the vomit to rise.

brigitte spits the little bit of vomit into the lavatory bowl. after that brigitte goes to her brassières as a new person, like a newborn person. through her new-born, she has the chance almost to be new born herself. there will also be a second construction of a livelihood.

now everything will be really cosy.

nature has turned birth and death in nature into a big secret. soon brigitte will know this secret.

birth and death, more exactly: the birth of brigitte's baby. the van driver parents will hopefully die as quickly as possible, otherwise they'll still have a long and difficult stay in an old people's home in front of them. because age has to make way for youth and its

energy. the van driver parents just don't know anything about their unpleasant fate yet.

apart from that heinz's boss and master should die
and kick the bucket as fast as possible too, because
heinz, who did his apprenticeship in the former's
small workshop, has qualified and needs his chance.
here he stands, the future business successor, is the
childless master blind?

heinz's hopes rise higher, heave-ho.

his whole small family will make dying easy for the
master, so that heinz can soon set up on his own.
one must vigorously modernise, renovate, paint and
expand, then everything is vigorously modernised,
renovated, painted and enlarged.

so the old must make way for the young, and brigitte
makes way in her stomach for something newer,
better, more beautiful, then what was previously lying
around in there unused.

the little child will occupy an important place:
inheritor of the business! brigitte will occupy the
second most important place: worker in the shop and
in the home.

until now brigitte has occupied an unimportant
place: worker in a women's underwear factory. that
is one rung lower, no, several rungs.

and then came the day on which she tells heinz.
brigitte confesses her secret to heinz.

heinz had been afraid of this the whole time, but
now he can't shirk it. a gentleman does not shirk his
duty.

before i pay for the child, i at least want some work
from the mother on behalf of the shop, he says in a
smart-ass way to his completely stunned family, who
cling to one another as if in a storm.

an illusion called susi falls away from the van driver father.

an illusion called susi falls away from the van driver mother.

soon the fruit will fall from the trees, and the parents will have to leave the house, to make way for the next generation. their savings book stays here.

daddy's discs ache and his heart aches. suddenly father has a second ache in his old age.

however: the alliance of business and culture (susi) has once again failed to take place.

heinz's business spirit stands alone.

his momma too had similar cultural plans, which now she must abandon. what a nice couple they would have made, little susi all in white and her heinzi, all in black! is there a contrast richer in contrast?

is there anything, that is simultaneously so different and yet in such harmony? or would have been?

and then children, whom their mummy could help with their homework, who one day could learn about the business from the bottom up . . .

it was not to be. brigitte provides no contrast to heinz, brigitte is like heinz only far beneath him.

a somewhat simpler person.

heinz feels brigitte's pregnancy to be a constraint, which one can ultimately put to good use.

there will be a marriage.

brigitte walks around as if on a cloud and believes, that in her condition she is something special and has to be looked after.

brigitte is right.

brigitte's off season begins.

soon the underwear line will come to a stop for brigitte.

that's a blessing words can hardly describe.

instead of stiff nylon borders now soft little woollen jackets slip through brigitte's maternal fingers. there is great pride in brigitte at her achievement.

she has undergone a process from an incomplete hybrid form of being to a female being.

even heinz's old master is as happy as a senile idiot because of the baby. he says, that it's good that there's new blood again, that's still fresh, he doesn't talk about handing over the business. old fool.

the old master leaves no room for doubt, that he is still master here and will remain so.

heinz leaves brigitte no room for doubt, as to who is boss now. brigitte is so happy, to have a boss at last. if one has been without a boss for so long, it is a relief to find a good little boss.

heinz's mummy is happy about the child. she knits and knits senselessly away like a madwoman. she can do that. she can do that, without having learned it. because she didn't learn anything anyway.

heinz's daddy grumbles it is true, like an old daddy always grumbles in the cinema and on tv, but as in the cinema and on tv he doesn't really mean it.

brigitte looks after her stomach, along with her stomach brigitte herself is looked after too. it does her good.

susi congratulates them. susi wishes them the very best.

heinz and brigitte thank her. brigitte says we're going to marry soon. before there's anything to be seen.

now i have to look after myself and prepare for the

little child in peace and quiet. brigitte eavesdrops on herself, but hears no echo.

susi says, she never wants to have children, i.e. later some day certainly, when she is more mature and has relieved the hunger in the world, in the meantime she wants to put off having children, because first she wants to see the world and the hunger in it, now she is still too young. once she has seen the world, she wants perhaps to go for a year as an aid worker to one of the dark places in this world. and then perhaps she'll marry too, and when the right man comes along, she wants to have children too.

susi is waiting for her great love, which she still (little smile) believes in.

what susi does not say, but what she thinks about, is a young graduate, who, if he were to appear on the horizon right now, would find susi's heart and hand as well as her little susi pussy as wide open as a barn door.

meanwhile susi is not yet ready, girlish, flowery and walled up. she is still waiting like a closed poppy, corn or sunflower on someone, who will open her up. with a rose bouquet full of roses.

susi also says, that to be a woman alone is not enough, one must use women's female characteristics for what they were intended: to care and look after and in the widest sense to help.

susi gives advice free of charge and tax free for brigitte's new life. heinz also adds the usual allusions to his new captured, bound status, but in a jolly and coarsely humorous manner, as is his way. susi screws up her eyes in shock, because heinz is vulgar. heinz feels himself more than ever a man, which he is too.

good-humouredly brigitte leads heinz away from susi, from the latent danger, which has at last been defused. good-humouredly she points out, that heinz will soon be a husband and a father now. no more strange girls. both approach their wedding good-humouredly. susi thinks good-humouredly, he really did believe, he could get me, whereas only someone much much better can get me.

brigitte thinks good-humouredly, now i and not little susi have got the very best.

the family good-humouredly allude to fat stomach and millstone around one's neck. today everyone is in a good mood. and in the evening there's the good-humoured perry como show.

brigitte feels as if she is in a warm bath.

the WEDDING

today the longed-for day has come at last. glorious blue skies greet the much longed-for day. today the longed-for day has come at last. glorious blue skies greet the much longed-for day.

brigitte is wearing a floor length white dress, which the dressmaker sewed just for her.

paula is wearing a floor length white dress, which the dressmaker, her former employer, sewed just for her.

brigitte has a bouquet of white roses on her arm.

paula has a bouquet of white roses on her arm.

heinz is wearing a black suit with a bow tie.

erich is wearing a new black suit with a nice tie.

heinz continually makes silly jokes about his lost freedom.

many jokes are cracked about erich and about his lost freedom.

heinz talks about his future business, brigitte supports him as he does so, she puts her hand possessively on his.

erich things about his engines, paula thinks, that once again she had a narrow escape.

brigitte is grateful, paula is grateful.

brigitte thinks, that she certainly will stick up for herself sometimes, but on the whole heinz is right, and she'll do, what he says.

paula thinks, that from now on she will only do, what erich tells her.

brigitte has at last found a real complement to her life: a partner for richer for poorer.

paula has at last found a real complement to her life: a partner for richer or poorer.

many relatives have come to heinz and brigitte's wedding.

many relatives have come to erich and paula's wedding.

the wedding of heinz and brigitte is very moving and solemn.

the wedding of erich and paula is very moving and solemn.

brigitte is very happy.

paula is very happy.

brigitte has made it.

paula has made it.

brigitte is pregnant and will soon be able to hold her child in her arms.

paula already has a baby. she has already been holding it in her arms for a while. but today the baby must stay at home.

heinz is now master in the house, as he says good-humouredly.

erich is now master in the house, as he cannot formulate, but as others whisper to him.

heinz drinks a couple of glasses of wine and becomes jovial and says, that he is now master in the house, and that his parents might as well kick the bucket, but he expresses it more delicately. his poor old parents are the first people to be unhappy in this cheerful company.

erich once again drinks himself into a stupor and can say nothing at all any more. paula is nevertheless still happy in this joyful company.

heinz's parents pay for the wedding reception grumbling and making snide remarks, brigitte's mother adds something as well, which is too little however, heinz's parents make snide remarks about brigitte's background.

paula's parents happily pay for the wedding reception. now no one can look down on them any more.

later there's dancing.

later there's dancing.

that applies in both cases.

what is being celebrated, is, that at last a woman and a man are entering the house.

brigitte and heinz will live in the little summer house of heinz's parents, until they can worry and build heinz's parents out of house and home, enlarge and fit out house and shop.

paula and erich will get a little room with paula's parents, until they can afford a small apartment or even build one!

now brigitte and heinz must save and save again. because setting up a home costs money!

now erich must save and save again. because setting up a home costs money!

both women have to save their husbands' money.

heinz and brigitte will succeed at that.

erich and paula will not succeed at that.

an electrician earns quite a good wage.

a woodcutter earns a poor wage.

erich drinks.

heinz drinks only rarely and in moderation.

erich drinks almost everything away.

heinz doesn't drink anything away, because he is ambitious and sensible.

with brigitte and heinz things work out so well, that soon they will have driven their parents and parents-in-law out of the house.

with brigitte and heinz things are going so well, that they will have a little boy as well: harry.

with paula and erich things are going badly. one year later they will have a boy as well: karl.

in the meantime however we still want to dance light-heartedly at brigitte and heinz's wedding.

in the meantime however we still want to dance light-heartedly at erich and paula's wedding.

and enjoy the beautiful day.

and enjoy the beautiful day.

paula has tied her fate to erich, who will hang like a millstone around her neck.

brigitte has tied her fate to heinz, which was the right thing to do and will bring her a shop of her own as well as a nice car.

by chance paula has had bad luck and will suffer a terrible downfall.

by chance brigitte has been lucky and will experience a meteoric rise.

brigitte invested a lot, all the resources of her body and mind.

paula invested a lot, all the resources of her body and mind.

brigitte finds happiness and success.

paula does not find happiness and success.

brigitte's happiness depends on chance, which smiles on her.

paula's happiness depends on chance, which does not smile on her.

heinz has a job with a future.

erich has a job without a future, but with a solid present.

heinz knows, what matters in the world of business.

erich doesn't have a clue, what matters in the world of business. erich knows, what matters in the world of grand prix motor racing: a fast car.

heinz knows, that he is well informed. heinz knows, that his wife is not well informed. heinz has power over his uninformed wife.

erich is not well informed. he nevertheless has unlimited power over his wife, which he will make the most of.

the dreams of brigitte and heinz look just like paula's dreams.

erich has no dreams apart from the dreams about his engines.

but erich has alcohol.

the dreams of brigitte and heinz will come true.

paula's dreams will not come true.

erich will not get his driving licence either, which will hit him hard, but will perhaps prolong his life.

so each of the four people who are so happy today will have their cross to bear.

after all property is responsibility.
no property means no responsibility.
however paula's cross will be no lighter for that.
today two non-owners of property and two owners
of property with a promising future have got married.

oh, must i then, must i then leave the little house . . . (the parents leave the nest)

the years came and went and children became
people.
heinz developed as he had wished, he developed into
a first class businessman, who did the work just
where it was needed and where he subsequently also
held his own. his wife sold electrical appliances in
the shop. but they had saved hard for it, worked and
taken out loans. for that they worked, saved and took
out further loans. they worked and saved hard.
it had all happened exactly as brigitte had wished
and imagined. she had a sweet child and a second
was already on the way. what else did they need to
be content? they needed nothing else to be content,
but no, wait, there was something they needed to be
content: that something was more space in their new
spick and span little house.
and there was something else they would have wished
for: that there's ever more of everything and it constantly gets bigger. and so everything continues to
grow and constantly gets bigger.
and one day it came too, the much longed-for day:
in the garden leaves were already turning colourful
and autumnal, the michaelmas daisies and the dahlias were already flowering, the sun gilded the apples

and pears on the branches, which would soon be ripe, the birds were already flying south, where they would remain for a while, and there stood heinz's old parents also ready to move out with their chests, boxes and suitcases, there they stood now at the door of their enlarged little house, in which they had been happy side by side for so many years, in which they had raised little heinzi to be a hardworking adult person, in which they had made him into an independent person, which he had indeed become, an independent businessman, in which they had further sown and reaped, always more sown than reaped, and apart from that they had also seen the seasons come and go there, received letters and written cards and spent many a twilight hour in front of television and beer.

there stood these storm-lashed old folks, ready to move into a small but inhuman one-room apartment, to make space for the young people, to whom the world and in it of course the rebuilt and enlarged family house now belongs. off to the one-room apartment, the antechamber to the old peoples' home. was that a leavetaking, a toing and froing and a waving goodbye! quick quick, we have to go.

once more the grandchild was picked up, once more the lad was hugged and squeezed, once more the daughter-in-law sized up with poisoned poisonous glances and found wanting, once more their former kingdom fixed in their glances of farewell, the garden and the rock garden (the alpinium), the cluster of pines and the rosebed. what would the young people unused to garden work make of it, would they let it run wild or would they care for it, as decent people do and as the van driver father despite his aches had never neglected to do??? does he not have tears in his eyes, does pa, and saliva in the corner of his mouth, which secretly and unobserved he wipes away? does mummsy too not have a heavy heart?

no, the young people mustn't notice anything, they must build their own lives unhindered just as they want to, we old people don't want to stand in their way!

it's just that brigitte has completely ruined our heinzi. without gitti we would still be here today and would plant, till, sow and mow, but with gitti, we're being torn away from our little grandchild, the joy and pride of our old age.

but we'll visit you very often, harry! do you like it when granny and grandad come? and harald beams and says yes and will you always bring me something? touched, granny promises to do so, she who still cannot come to terms at all with life in the smelly city, no trees any more, no grass, no flowers, no savings account any more, only hard cold lonely dreary concrete desert. for miles.

and not a soul, with whom one can have a little chat.

not a soul, who is human and friendly in this concrete block. that this had to happen to us in our old age.

but the young people are right.

but harald is a fine lad. one day he will inherit and take over father's shop. what his father has built up, the lad can make even bigger. the foundation's there.

don't squander your inheritance, when the time comes, don't squander it, harald, don't you dare.

it's true your mummy is a tramp, who has ruined our heinzi for us, but your daddy will make sure, that one day you'll be a hard-working man, because he is a hard-working man himself. and grandad can teach you too, what a man has to know, how to climb up trees and make a catapult to shoot birds, how to play with the railway and not to cry like a lassie if one cuts one's knee, grandad will come to visit very often and look after the garden a little, because the young people don't have much time for that, and granny will often come too, and when grandad is here, he'll show you, how to grow up to be a proper big man, harald!

because grandad is a man too, you know.

an impatient heinz, who has to get away to an installation job and will soon take on a craftsman, thinks that the old arsehole should finally get a move on out of the house, because otherwise he'll give him a helping hand, he's going to lose his temper in a minute. the old bum can come as often as he likes, but now he should just get a move on and leave, visit us, just as often as you like, harald will be especially pleased as well as my wife and i, your son heinz. and inaudible: get lost now.

it is a very melancholy departure.

brigitte, the mistress of the house, who is at the moment busy with the housework, comes to say goodbye. she has become a clean, a somewhat plump little woman. the marriage is filling her out, one can see that. she beams in competition with the baking tins. hate has quite eaten her up inside. but the pleasure of ownership has remained. she clings to it with an iron fist.

filled with hate, brigitte, wife and mother, who has meanwhile cleaned millions of shit pans, takes her leave of the parents-in-law. alone at last. at last the

car has driven off. at last the family is alone and can
lead a family life as a proper family should.

heinz and brigitte begin their family life right away,
in which every day is the same and means work work
work.

but work after all makes life sweet and is what life's
about. that's what the old parents leave to the young
people as legacy and inheritance, that together with
their savings, which have gone into the house and
shop.

once more brigitte enfolds her little kingdom, which
will soon be enlarged even further – the last word
has not yet been spoken and will be spoken by heinz
– with her gaze and all her other senses, then with a
sigh she goes into the house, driving little harry
before her with kicks.

daddy has already gone.

harry cannot speak properly yet, sometimes he is also
hugged and kissed, he likes that much better.

and chocolate, sweeties and biscuits even more.

daddy is away on his installation job, mummy sells a
drainage outlet made of high grade steel, because it's
better than the ordinary kind.

mummy sells in addition a hairdryer, two small elec-
tric convector heaters and one of the new bathroom
mirrors with a light attached. mummy can be satisfied with her day, because it was a good one.

good days come more and more often now.

and so an inner contentment has at last come to this
woman.

susi, the chatterbox who needn't be taken seriously,
is supposed to have a student boyfriend now. susi too
will accept the fate of a woman as brigitte has

accepted it. brigitte, smart girl, recognised the fate of a woman even before susi.

brigitte's fate was the jackpot, she can't complain, brigitte managed it all with the strength of her womb alone. many a strong man needs much more strength than that.

but then what is our women's charm for anyway?

hence the chapter title: must I then must I then . . .

and what does paula have? paula has a kingdom too

at this time paula surveyed her little kingdom too.

paula's little kingdom consists of a little room, in her parents' little house. there paula holds sway.

she holds sway over her older and her younger child. her husband erich holds sway over paula.

squabbling and quarrelling can often poison a family's whole life with their poisonous breath.

erich and paula's family life is often poisoned by the poisonous breath of squabbling and quarrelling. despite the risk of poisoning erich and paula go on squabbling and quarrelling.

nevertheless erich is my husband after all, thinks paula. she tries very hard to create a good atmosphere, so that the children can grow up in peace and quiet and she herself can grow into a woman in peace and quiet.

today for example paula has been invited to a dance in the neighbouring village. can I go to this dance, paula already asks excitedly three days before. yes, when you've taken care of the children, you can go, promises erich. the children will be taken by momma.

today is the day of the party, on which paula puts her hair in curlers. when erich came home, he immediately asked paula where she intended going, whereupon the latter replied she was going to the dance in the neighbouring village with her girlfriend and her husband. it's the first time that paula can go out.

but now erich suddenly says no, i won't allow it.

paula cries. paula cries heartbreakingly like a child. despite that she is not allowed to go dancing. paula acted up for a long time afterwards and pulled a face but erich was unrelenting. because on this issue he didn't stand for any nonsense.

but at the happy laughter of her children paula couldn't remain unhappy for long.

now paula has the firm structure, which she wanted. she has a place in a structure and is not the unplaced part. paula knows her place. there are cogwheels, turning all around her which she fits between.

erich has at last got power over a person, even if it's as insignificant a figure as paula. there is now some-one, who does, what erich says. erich has the right to forbid or allow something. it's a new feeling, which he makes the most of. sometimes even with unreasonable orders.

what paula wishes for, is a little home of her own at last.

what paula wishes for, is a little home of her own at last in which she can do as she pleases just like brigitte.

squabbling and quarrelling will not be allowed in there.

on the threshold paula will bar their way and say: stay outside hate squabbling and quarrelling, this is my home!

since paula's home is not her own and in addition spatially very limited, peace and quiet cannot call in here, but must turn back at the threshold.

although it was proven long ago, that quarrelling can destroy any community. erich drinks, which paula will also stop, as soon as she has crossed the threshold of the new home, which one cannot afford, however, because erich drinks. alcohol will stay outside together with the squabbles and the quarrels.

the heavy physical work will however cross the threshold without inhibition and stay there.

in this one little room sleep and live husband and wife.

the children sleep with granny, her own husband has not slept with her for a long time, he sleeps in the attic.

when paula, children dangling from her, goes shopping, she sometimes briefly envies the formerly despised sales assistants for their purity and cleanliness. with an effort paula also keeps up her former purity and cleanliness, the only thing left to her, which was always her greatest attraction. it takes much more effort than before. she also has to keep a man clean, who again and again pukes over himself and sometimes even pisses himself.

an alcoholic's wife has to be able to do that, those are the basic qualifications. laughter is heard in the village, erich likes his wine better than any woman ha ha.

in reality erich likes his wine much better than his wife paula, even if he also perhaps loves the children more than his wine. he often buys them an ice cream. they can say please please so nicely.

erich still loves his engines.

one day paula takes her driving test. she passes it right away first time. that makes erich happy, because it brings a car into the house. and right, instead of the hoped for apartment it brings a secondhand renault into the house.

the renault gives paula a lift and a new high point. she can now drive around in a car, which she is not allowed to do, however, except when erich is with her.

she is one of the few women in the village, who has a driving licence. paula is only allowed to drive the car, when erich is sitting beside her and making loud engine noises.

one day paula even got to italy on holiday with erich and the new car, for a large part of the long journey erich made droning noises.

the children stayed with the parents.

that was a beautiful high point. it was the high point of paula's life so far.

after the high point the couple came back again. here they were not strangers as in italy, here they were at home. right away paula started hoping for a new apartment again. but in vain.

soon paula sank back into the daily round again.

soon erich sank back again into forest, into wine and into beer.

but the children are sweet and good and always do what they're told.

their momma-in-law, their momma, their mummy and their daddy make sure of that. they jump to every word and sometimes even before.

it is a real joy for paula, to have such good and healthy children. how can one have any selfish interests, when one has such sweet sensible children, say the village people.

when the little girl breaks her arm one day, paula can even drive her to the hospital in the county town in her own car. erich understands, why this time paula took the car without his permission. this is by no means the beginning of a learning process for erich.

slowly the work in the forest has destroyed and obliterated a large part of erich's former good looks, just as it has almost destroyed the skin on his hands. the female summer visitors hardly ever turn round to look at him any more. one can hardly tell erich apart from the other woodcutters any more. he has also become noticeably more apathetic.

paula too has become a rather more apathetic person than she was, although she even enjoys the housework.

what paula does not have, is a little pleasure and even less tenderness, nevertheless paula is still happy that she has a fixed place in life and that she has children. she wants things to remain that way.

paula no longer things about dressmaking. and dressmaking no longer thinks about paula. another apprentice from the larger nearby town took her place, and after *her* another one.

the eyes of the village rest on paula as they rest on all the others whose lives are well ordered and bounded. the eyes of the village make sure, that none of the boundaries is crossed.

since paula behaves in accordance with the rules of the owners of the village eyes, she is registered as a necessary evil, but remains undisturbed and unmentioned, does not stand out from the other female inhabitants.

paula's efforts with erich have been taken note of without good will, her efforts in the fight against alcohol and physical decline have been observed with faint amusement, the way one looks at the jokes in the sunday paper, provided one gets them. her particular cleanliness and well groomed appearance are not commented on at all any more, because they are familiar, and it's accepted, that she has children like the rest.

everything is in order.

paula is really quite happy, but she would still like to have a place of her own, where she can realise her profession: housewife and mother. there is no money for that.

paula should not want to get above her obstinate little self complains the serialised novel.

if paula had remained sensible in the spirit of the serialised novel, she would not have strayed onto the path which was to be her ruin.

the place, where paula was to end up, was the crooked path.

the place, where erich has always remained and still remains today, is the straight and narrow path. the forest and the inn.

the village and the serialised novel say, that the wife must watch over the hearth at home, must protect it, and not throw any dirt into it.

for a short time paula did not watch over and protect it, paula threw dirt onto the hearth at home.

that will cost paula her head.

and yet another engagement

the master craftsman's diploma hangs in a frame on the wall of brigitte and heinz's electrical goods shop.

today an engagement is also being celebrated in the house of susi's parents. he is a young secondary school teacher. in the circle around the young couple there are enthusiastic discussions, which sometimes even turn quite serious.

no mindless amusement.

in susi's opinion mindless brigitte bears a triple burden as woman mother and businesswoman.

clever susi only bears a double burden: woman and mother (soon). she has given up studying german, which she has just begun, she is expecting a baby shortly.

both women flourish under their new responsibilities.

both women flourish under their new responsibilities.

heinz flourishes under brigitte's cooking. he is already as fat as a pig, that is his physical predisposition anyway. heinz tends to corpulence. brigitte's cooking skills are often the subject of jokes.

heinz's skills as a businessman are never the subject of any jokes whatsoever. they are serious and existential.

gitti too has already acquired a charming feminine plumpness, a little potbelly. brigitte's plumpness serves to say: a happy businesswoman, housewife and mother.

she possesses a degree of equanimity, which she also scatters around her. susi on the other hand wants to stay slim with gymnastics, so as to be and remain a good lover for her husband. she also wants to stay

mentally fit. she intends, to continue reading many
good books and perhaps also to round off her knowledge of foreign languages. this young couple too
wants to build something.

susi also wants to be an intellectual partner. it's also
good for the children, if the mother's mind is ticking
over.

heinz's parents don't look well at all. they miss the
garden and the fresh air in it. they also miss their
grandchildren. their children and children-in-law
(one of each) show intolerance and a lack of understanding for these problems.

they would like to come to visit now and then,
which they neither should nor are allowed to. the van
driver's account is empty, and that's fine. it was all
for the children, for whom one lives after all. there
is not enough for a nice holiday any more.

gitti lives for the children and the business. the
business lives for heinz. surely he won't have a girlfriend?

but no. mamma, as brigitte is called now, makes
good food, which is easily even more tempting than
a distant unknown and uncertain adventure.

sure, mamma's good food is even more tempting
than an adventure, one of heinz's female cousins asks
her cousin heinz for a joke with a sidelong glance at
brigitte. heinz replies for a joke, that an adventure
certainly is tempting, but everyone here knows that
it's a lie, and so everybody is satisfied.

susi too has very much enjoyed cooking since she
was young, but only fancy, high class cooking which
also includes diet foods and specialities from abroad,
and which doesn't make one fat, which is not
modern.

susi is a more modern woman, brigitte a rather old fashioned one, but lovable.

but that's just how heinz likes brigitte. he really doesn't want her any different.

he wouldn't know what to do with a modern woman.

so they've all become happy contented people, who take their place in life and take up even more. heinz, if he keeps on eating like that, will soon be able to take up two places.

but that is only a good-natured joke.

the two places and more, which heinz already takes up in his head, he will soon also be able to take up in life in person.

today there's roast pork and dumplings.

susi says jokingly, but good-naturedly, that she is satisfied, with the place she now occupies in life, that she wouldn't like to change places with anybody, who perhaps gets an outstanding degree and then fails at life.

susi is modern and old fashioned at once, a combination, which her fresh young fiancé is especially fond of.

in any case: a sensible middle course is always best, says susi much more seriously, than one would expect from her pretty little head.

and her future spouse agrees with a laugh.

how paula allows herself to be carried away

we don't know, what went on in paula's head, the day she strayed from the straight and narrow.

was it the desire for money, the desire for a modest affluence, which led her to the place, where she suffered her fall? or was it unrestrained sexual desire, which her husband erich should have fulfilled for her? and indeed erich before anyone else!

so was it the sexuality in paula or was it her desire for security or was it her desire for a security that could be bought with money, for an apartment of her own?

the village would like to know, but is dependent on conjecture. it is a fact, that paula did some disgusting things. these disgusting things put an end to all security, which proved, that security cannot be bought with money. one can only earn security by patience and perseverance. although paula has loved patiently and perseveringly for years, she had not got any security yet.

all devious methods, of getting a man and then holding him are welcomed here.

paula's method, of holding her man and providing him with a cosy home, which he and her children would have earned, but which erich cannot pay for, was rejected and condemned here. paula's method was a disgrace, and she got her just reward for it.

but I only did it for the children and for erich, paula may have said, but nobody was listening to her.

the facts speak their own language and for themselves.

when a man's pride is injured, then it is difficult to make good again. a woman doesn't even need to bother with pride.

paula didn't even introduce pride into her life either. one day paula drove secretly to the county town, nobody knows why, it was to go to the cinema and the café, which don't exist in the village. paula believes, that's part of life, that's wrong. for lack of time we can no longer allow paula in person a chance to speak here.

when paula parked at the railway station, a stranger bent down to her window and asked her: how about it, why don't we go and kiss a bit?

at first paula said no look i'm married and have two cute children.

but then paula agreed, to drive a little way with the man, to a secluded place.

we do not know, what at this moment took place in paula's head, from which dressmaking had already been banished years ago and into which erich and the children had already moved some time ago.

something wrong took place in paula's head.

for a long time nothing has happened in paula's snatch any more. if one doesn't feel anything, that's very far from meaning it never happened.

paula did it for her family.

perhaps in this way paula can give her family a fixed abode. it's a miracle that paula held out so long without one. since at 15 she already dreamt of nothing else but this abode, of white curtains and shiny household appliances. security also requires one's own four walls and a roof over it.

perhaps it's paula's chance to build a nest. paula wants to copy the swallows: build a nest. so goes a popular song from an operetta.

paula must not make anything, which she is not entitled to.

erich has to make the home.

and feminine means are unsuitable means in order to produce anything.

i love my husband, says paula to this man and to the

next one and to the one after that. and can you give
me a little money?

and paula gets given a little money.

i'd like to earn my daily bread as easily as that, erich
may have thought.

paula doesn't think, that money, which she suddenly
has, needs to be noticed. she only wants to save.
operation squirrel. she also spends a little in the café.
one day paula wants to make a down payment on an
apartment.

paula acquires with her body and without her mind
the means to purchase a small apartment.

what paula is doing is prostitution. paula is a whore.
she takes money from strange men, and then in the
car, on the back seat or in the grass a strange man
pokes into her, what only erich is allowed to poke
into her. the wrong thing in the wrong place. it is an
amateurish undertaking.

one should organise something like that on a larger
scale.

paula should have known, that she can't achieve anything with an object like her body. paula has not
learnt anything new since her brief youth.

paula's body doesn't fail her it is true, it willingly
does its duty. the world around however refuses
paula's body its good will.

the world around is suddenly witness to this act in a
copse.

the driver of a forestry truck, who only wanted to go
for a piss, just at that place of all places, where nor-
mally nobody ever pisses, apart from a little deer or
a little hare, had been able to see the half-naked
lower part of paula's body working with a man who
was not her husband. he said, that the two of them

were intertwined and interlocked in a disgusting way.

he repeats it again very often.

apart from that he knew paula's name and address.

he saw, that what paula was up to here in the middle of innocent nature, was a betrayal of his friend erich.

paula has betrayed her husband. paula has betrayed her husband with another or several other men.

on top of that he was not a local man. not one of the lads from round here. a stranger has been fouling their nest.

yuk. and a mother with two children of her own and who's on the pill now.

it was a betrayal of his friend erich!

paula's neck should be broken or she should be sterilised at least, so that she can't have any more children, to whom she can pass on her hereditary dispositions.

paula is more of a bad bitch than a bitch on heat, which can't fight against it out of instinct.

paula's neck was broken but she wasn't sterilised. it could have been worse.

apart from that erich divorced paula as the guilty party.

although it wasn't paula's intention, her marriage broke down on the spot after her frequent lapses.

although it was by no means paula's intention, her happiness broke into pieces at the same time as her marriage.

although paula thought very hard against it, she herself broke into pieces.

although paula made feeble attempts to prevent it, her whole social framework broke into pieces on top of all the other ruins as well.

if only she had thought twice, because now it's too late! if paula had guessed, what would break in pieces, as a result of her admittedly considered but mistaken marriage transgression, she would never even have started with the breaking.

it happened with the force of a spring avalanche.

here one lives on intimate terms with nature, one cannot resist it because it's stronger.

erich too suffers a great deal, perhaps he'll never get over it, says his momma.

but the children mustn't suffer too much because of the filth the mother got up to, pleads momma-in-law.

the children suffer terribly because of the filth the mother got up to, because suddenly they hardly ever see their dear mummy any more, really virtually never.

they ask why and don't understand. it's unfortunate, that the poor little things don't understand yet. when they're old enough, they'll understand. probably they won't really understand.

it'll be up to them then, whether they condemn or don't condemn their momma, says one of erich's more intelligent workmates, who can also express himself in words.

the children now live with paula's parents in the former room of the former married couple.

erich sells his ex-wife's car. it is a sad event. considering they spent their second honeymoon in italy, considering they might have been able to buy a little sports car one day. now he's only got the moped.

the moped sometimes takes him to his new girlfriend, a rich farmer's daughter who lives nearby. but he likes his glass of wine better than any woman, so that this burgeoning relationship will also probably founder soon.

perhaps women are also different now from what they used to be.

there are also hardly any folk dance groups any more.

that's a shame for susi above all.

paula started the breaking, now she is completely broken.

the girl in the first year of her dressmaking apprenticeship, who was full of hope, has become a broken woman with inadequate dressmaking skills.

that is too little.

epilogue:

do you know this BEAUTIFUL land with its valleys and hills?

in the distance it is bounded by beautiful mountains. it has a horizon, which is something many lands do not have.

do you know the meadows and fields of this land? do you know its peaceful houses and their peaceful inhabitants?

right in the middle of this beautiful land good people have built a factory. its low corrugated aluminium roof makes a beautiful contrast to the deciduous and coniferous forests all around. the factory is tucked into the landscape.

although there is no reason for it to be tucked away.

it could display itself. how fortunate that it stands here, in beautiful surroundings and not somewhere else, where the surroundings are not beautiful.

the factory looks as if it were part of this beautiful landscape.

it looks as if it had grown here, but no! if one looks at it more closely, one sees: good people built it. nothing comes of nothing after all.

and good people go in and out of it.

is this good person, who goes in and out here, not our paula?

stop, good morning, paula! really, it is her. outwardly she's hardly changed, still slim and clean. except there's a weary undertone in her face, which one only sees however, if one looks more closely. and this wrinkle. was it there yesterday?

no, it's a new wrinkle. and that wouldn't be a grey

hair would it? doesn't matter, paula, just keep your chin up!

paula works here as an unskilled seamstress on the assembly line.

paula works here as an unskilled seamstress on the assembly line.

paula has finished up in the place from which brigitte set out, to get to know life. brigitte has got to know life and found her happiness in it.

paula wanted to get to know life too, now she's getting to know the job of a semi-skilled worker in an underwear factory.

that too is a kind of life.

in the evening the people pour into the landscape, as if it belonged to them.

paula now has a small apartment, which also belongs to the factory and is therefore cheap.

paula does less than a happy person, because she is unhappy.

nevertheless her work is satisfactory, the factory is patient.

there is no trace of impatience in paula any more.

paula has come to this place to sew, not to be happy. she could have been happy before.

now she unhappily sews foundations, brassières, corsets and panties. paula married and was ruined.

never does her gaze wander outside to a bird, a bee or a blade of grass. paula has had enough of birds, bees and blades of grass. but in those days she was unable to value them properly.

any man can enjoy nature better than paula today.

paula sits at her sewing machine and performs her duty. she has a lot of responsibility, but no broad view and no household any more.

in the evening she drives home to her little apartment and thinks about home. paula is too tired to be discontented.

paula has no children and no husband any more, nevertheless, she is too tired to be discontented about that.

once paula had a husband and two children.

nor does the work make paula discontented.

the work makes paula apathetic.

sewing is in paula's blood. only she let this blood out long ago, that's why she is not as good at her work as the others. which means deductions.

paula sews with all her heart, because she has no family any more, which could take up part of her heart.

now brigitte has a family and a business, which have taken up all of her heart.

it is not the very best women, who sew with all their heart.

paula is not the very best woman.

paula has already experienced her fate somewhere else. here it is over.

brigitte began her fate here. brigitte has got away.

paula was struck down. if life happens to be passing by, paula doesn't try to speak to it. she doesn't care to chat any more.

there goes life, paula!

but our paula is still looking for her car keys.

goodbye, and safe journey, paula.

Also by Elfriede Jelinek and published by Serpent's Tail

Wonderful, Wonderful Times

Translated by Michael Hulse

'That's brutal violence on a defenceless person, and quite unnecessary, declares Sophie, and she pulls with an audible tearing sound at the hair of the man lying on an untidy heap on the ground. What's unnecessary is best of all, says Rainer, who wants to go on fighting. We agreed on that.'

It is the late 1950s. A man is out walking in a park in Vienna. He will be beaten up by four teenagers, not for his money, he has an average amount – nor for anything he might have done to them, but because arrogance is their way of reacting to the maggot-ridden corpse that is Austria where everyone has a closet to hide their Nazi histories, their sexual perversions and their hatred of the foreigner. Elfriede Jelinek, who wites like an angel of all that is tawdry, shows in *Wonderful, Wonderful Times* how actions of the present are determined by thoughts of the past.

'A dozen years after the collapse of the Third Reich, four adolescents commit a gratuitously violent assault and robbery in a Viennese park. So begins Jelinek's brilliant new novel, an unrelenting and horrifying exploration of postwar Austria' *Publishers Weekly*

'The writing is so strong, it reads as if it wasn't written down at all, but as if the author's demon spirit is entering first a boy and then a girl, a structure, a thing, a totality, to let it speak its horrible truth' *The Scotsman*

The Piano Teacher

Translated by Joachim Neugroschel

Erika Kohut teaches piano at the Vienna Conservatory by day. But by night she trawls the porn shows of Vienna while her mother, whom she loves and hates in equal measure, waits up for her.

Into this emotional pressure-cooker bounds music student and ladies' man, Walter Klemmer. With Walter as her student, Erika spirals out of control, consumed by the ecstasy of self-destruction.

First published in 1983, *The Piano Teacher* is the masterpiece of Elfriede Jelinek, Austria's most famous writer. Directed by Michael Haneke, the film won three major prizes at the Cannes 2001 Festival, including best actor for Benoît Magimel and best actress for Isabelle Huppert.

'A disturbing tale of love, fear and self-destruction . . . in this demented love story, the hunter is the hunted, pain is pleasure, and spite and self-contempt seep from every pore' *The Guardian*

'Draws its disturbing power from what it says about female sexuality' *Sunday Herald*

'A bravura performance, translated into vivid, flowing colloquial American-English, in which . . . the bleak landscape is lit by flashes of irony' Shena Mackay

'A brilliant, deadly book' Elizabeth Young

Lust

Translated by Michael Hulse

In a quaint Austrian ski resort, things are not quite what they seem.

Hermann, the manager of a paper mill, has decided that sexual gratification begins at home. Which means Gerti – his wife and property. Gerti is not asked how she feels about the use Hermann puts her to. She is a receptacle into which Hermann pours his juices, nastily, briefly, brutally.

The long-suffering and battered Gerti thinks she has found her saviour and love in Michael, a student who rescues her after a day of vigorous use by her husband. But Michael is on his way up the Austrian political ladder, and he is, after all, a man.

In Elfriede Jelinek's *mitteleuropa*, love is as distant from sex as the Alps are from the sea, and the everyday mechanics of husband, wife, and child, become a loveless horror. Both a condemnation of the myth of romantic love and an angry defence of women's sexuality, *Lust* is pornography for pessimists.

A bestseller throughout Europe, *Lust* conforms Elfriede Jelinek as the most challenging writer – female or male – in Europe today. It is a dark, dazzling performance.

'Extraordinarily well-written, with many brilliant turns of phrase, this remains in my mind, as the most disturbing European novel I have read this year' Robert Carver, *New Statesman*